THE

LONG

SHORT

CUT

THE
LONG
SHORT
CUT

by Andrew Garve

HARPER & ROW, PUBLISHERS

NEW YORK

AND EVANSTON

THE

LONG

SHORT

CUT

I

AT TEN O'CLOCK on a cool March evening Michael Bliss returned to 15 Bampton Gardens, the large Victorian house in Hampstead where he lived. He left his gray Mercedes convertible in the street and walked with springy stride up the semicircular drive. He was a good-looking man in his early thirties, tall, slim, immaculately groomed and, at the moment, dinner-jacketed.

He paused at the table in the high chandelier-lit entrance hall to see if anything had come for him by the evening post. The various postmen all dumped their letters on the table for the tenants to sort out, saving themselves a three-story climb and a trek round ten flats. Sometimes they had little choice, when mail arrived with the house address on it and no flat number. There were two such letters at the moment, Bliss noticed—one for a Mr. Ertz, from Switzerland, and one for a Mr. Edwards, from Swansea. Now who were they? Neither of them was a resident. House guests of residents, perhaps? Or former guests? Or people just using the place? With postal arrangements so casual, and the front door of the building never locked, Bliss had often thought number 15 would make a splendid

accommodation address. Anyone could come in and
collect a letter and no one would bother. However, it
wasn't his business. Live and let live.

There were two letters for him; both, by the look of
them, bills. He pulled a face, and went on up to the
top-floor flat, number 10, which had a landing of its
own, and let himself in. The flat, converted from the
nursery quarters of some opulent nineteenth-century
merchant, was spacious, warm, and comfortably furnished. The thick walls and solid, close-carpeted floor
insured reasonable quiet. From the front windows
there was a view over trees and tennis courts; from
the back, where an old-fashioned fire escape spiraled
down to a walled garden, a much wider view over
northwest London. There were three rooms, one of
them a well-equipped study; a large bathroom; a modern kitchen, which Bliss used minimally; and a very
big walk-in store cupboard, under a sloping roof, that
opened out of the study. The apartment suited Bliss
admirably. It was attractive without being at all flashy,
it was conveniently situated for his haunts in central
London, and the tenants in the other flats were mostly
elderly people without families who kept themselves
to themselves. The fact that the house had no resident
porter was, from Bliss's point of view, an additional
advantage.

He poured himself some whiskey at the little bar
he'd had fitted up in the sitting room, added ice from
the fridge, and idly switched on the radio. A girl was
singing a song about a boy who'd been killed on his
motorbike and she wanted him to wait for her at
heaven's gate. He switched off with a shudder and
opened the bills. One was from his service garage, one

from his wine merchant. Both were for considerable amounts. He went into the study and looked through some other bills, totting them up. Altogether, they came to nearly three hundred pounds. Several had been running for some time and ought, Bliss thought, to be settled. In his line of business, where confidence was everything, he couldn't afford to be lax about his debts. He had his image to think of. A good, honest citizen, reliable, well-heeled, credit-worthy, and as well-behaved as a bachelor needed to be. He'd worked hard at that image. The flat, in its pleasant, respectable street, was right for it. So was the Mercedes—a quality job and a joy to drive, but not flamboyant. So were the clothes he wore—tailored in Savile Row, fashionable but not extravagant. The thing was to avoid extremes. That way you escaped unwelcome attention, inspired trust, and kept out of trouble.

With the bills in his hand Bliss crossed to his desk, unlocked a drawer, and took out his bank statements. Unlike most people, he had several bank accounts, not all of them in England—a precaution against the travel-allowance vagaries of politicians and the curiosity of tax inspectors. He quickly added up his credits. As he'd supposed, the position wasn't too healthy. When all his bills were paid, he'd be down to his last five thou. And five thou. was the figure he'd come to regard as the danger point, the amber light. Anything less than that, and his freedom of maneuver began to be restricted. . . . What it meant was that he'd have to start thinking about work again.

He didn't feel particularly worried by the situation. He had a sanguine temperament, and he knew his abilities. He'd been at this point many times before, and he'd always managed to fall on someone's feet. He began to review various little ploys, humming softly to himself. He often hummed when he was planning a coup or working out a problem—usually hymn tunes, the vestigial result of much compulsory chapel-going in his youth. This time it was "Fight the Good Fight."

He considered, for a fleeting moment, the possibilities of Lady B. She'd be good for any amount, on her own terms, but to Bliss, a man of spirit and independence, the role of gigolo to a titled hag was humiliating and unsavory. No, he could do better than Lady B. There was the widow in Bournemouth, whose faith in his financial judgment was equaled only by her wealth. She'd happily give him fifty thou. to invest for her—but that kind of operation usually brought a day of reckoning, requiring ultimate flight. There were, of course, several people he could blackmail. He quite enjoyed blackmail as a battle of wits, a test of nerve —but on the other hand he didn't like to cause people mental distress if it could be avoided. What else, then? Nothing very promising at the moment, it seemed. Only small-time stuff, and Bliss had the deepest contempt for small-timers—the little men who made ice coins for gas meters, forged half crowns, wrote checks that bounced, left hotels without paying. They not only got caught, they deserved to. No, what he needed was a new idea, a *big* idea, so that he could make a real killing. Something he'd get pleasure out of, as well as profit; something that would stretch his talents, something with a spice of danger and commensurate rewards. Something that would set him up for years, if not for life.

Well, he wouldn't make a killing by hanging about in his flat. He must meet people, people with big money. And the night was young. What about that gambling club off Park Lane that he'd been introduced to a couple of weeks before? The Queen of Hearts. It wouldn't do to become known as an habitué—bad for the image—but he could certainly allow himself a second visit. And something interesting might emerge.

He went into the bathroom, brushed up the wave in his dark hair, and briefly studied his appearance. Yes—very elegant. Spotless shirt front, black tie in a carefully asymmetrical bow, neatly folded silk handkerchief. Chin still smooth from his five o'clock shave. No changes needed for his man-about-town role. No problems in that role, either—it was the easiest act in his chameleon repertoire. Quiet assurance, polished manners, sophisticated, amusing talk. A slightly drawling public school accent, completely phony and a bit *vieux jeu* these days, but it still seemed to go down well. Especially with women.

He finished his whiskey, checked the wad of money in his wallet, and went down to the car.

There was no space to park in front of the club, but Bliss found room for the Mercedes in a quiet mews round the corner and walked back.

The Queen of Hearts, though technically a club, was in character and appearance more like a casino, and a casino deliberately modeled on classic Monte Carlo lines. Its interior was very plush, with a gilt-and-crimson decor, deep-pile carpets, a glitter of mirrors and chandeliers, and a lot of reproduction Louis Quinze furniture. It had a stately commissionaire on duty outside its revolving mahogany doors, and an inside staff resplendent in Ruritanian livery. No expense had been spared.

Bliss showed his card and sauntered into the "chemmy" room, sniffing the Havana-scented air. There were a lot of people gathered at the tables, playing or watching in a hushed cathedral atmosphere. Most of them were in evening dress. Bliss strolled around, glancing occasionally over someone's shoulder at the play but mostly inspecting the company. He identified a film starlet, a Labour peer, and a man who was enjoying transient fame as a TV personality. The Queen of Hearts was very much an "in" place just now. He saw no one he knew, no one who might provide him with a useful introduction to a credulous millionaire. He nodded to the owner of the club, Lou Savona, a bald, big-bellied man in a wine-colored dinner jacket and dark glasses. Savona was padding softly around with a brandy and soda in his hand, chatting nonchalantly to his friends while keeping a watchful eye on the spots where the big chips were going down.

For a quarter of an hour Bliss followed the fall of the cards and the slight changes of personnel at the tables. Apart from the play, which at times was tense, he found little to interest him. These people had come to gamble or watch others gamble, not to get into conversation with strangers. The women, in particular, seemed completely absorbed. Maybe the Queen of Hearts hadn't been such a good choice after all. He moved on, paused briefly at a baccarat table, and passed through into the roulette room. He might as well have a modest flutter, he decided, now that he was here. He collected fifty pounds' worth of chips and when a seat became vacant he took it.

He played with an air of cynical pessimism, which proved to be well justified. He tried various combinations, won a little, lost more. Roulette was really a frightful bore. He tried doubling up for a while, until zero ended a promising run on black. He was just thinking of calling it a night when the player on his left departed and a girl took the empty chair. Bliss gave her a neighborly smile, which she coolly returned. She was a blonde, extremely attractive, in her late twenties, he guessed. She was wearing a white dress whose simple cut revealed a lot of very attractive bosom and shoulder. She had an eye-catching solitaire diamond ring on her right hand, nothing on her left. She appeared to be unescorted.

Bliss continued to lose. The girl was making small, cautious bets and just about breaking even. She seemed, Bliss thought, more interested in his play than her own. Between games, they began to exchange comments.

"Curious how so many people go for the numbers that haven't turned up," Bliss said, as some large stakes were swept away. "On the principle that things must change, I suppose. Quite wrong, of course. It's like the weather. The better it is, the more likely that it'll go on being good. And vice versa."

The girl glanced pointedly at his much-diminished pile of chips. "*You* don't seem to be doing very well."

"I never do. Long on advice, short on achievement, that's me." It was the reverse of the truth, but it sounded snappy. "Anyway, I reckon this table's on a slope."

The croupier looked sharply at him, decided it was a joke, and called for the next game.

Bliss counted his remaining chips, cashed a check and bought some more. "I feel like plunging," he said. "You wouldn't like to suggest a number, would you?"

"All right," the girl said. "Seven."

Bliss stacked all his chips on seven. The wheel spun. The ball slotted in twenty-eight.

He smiled, shrugging off the loss. "Well, I guess that's that."

"You take it very well," the girl said.

"What do you expect me to do, go out and shoot myself? It's all in the game. I thought you might change my luck, but it seems you haven't."

She gave him a long, cool look. "Isn't it a bit early to judge?" she said.

Bliss eyed her speculatively. "Maybe it is. Perhaps you'd care to join me for a drink—they've a quite imaginative bar here. It would soften the blow."

"I'd be happy to," she said.

She got up, wafting a delicious scent around her, and set off through the crowd. Bliss, following a step behind her, noted the easy gracefulness of her walk. She had, he saw, beautiful legs.

In the bar, with the drinks set up, Bliss took a closer look at the rest of her, checking over her points with a connoisseur's eye. Ash-blond hair, shoulder length, with a long, loose wave, swept back over one ear—looked soft to the touch. Small, perfectly shaped nose. Exquisitely modeled mouth, its lovely line accentuated by the merest touch of a pale lipstick. Very large, wide-open blue eyes under long lashes that gave her a look of innocent surprise. About five feet six. Shapely all over. Pleasant low voice. Quite delicious . . .

He offered her a cigarette from his case, lit it for her with a snap of his gold lighter, and raised his glass. "Cheers . . . My name's Michael Bliss, by the way."

"Mine's Corinne Lake."

"M'm—that falls pleasantly on the ear. I don't think I ever knew a Corinne before."

"Aren't you sure?"

He laughed. "I guess I asked for that. . . . Tell me, do you often come here?"

"No, this is my first time." There was a slight pause. "I was supposed to be meeting a friend, but at the last minute he telephoned and said he had to fly to Los Angeles. I thought as I was already here I might as well stay and see what the place was like. I had to take out membership, of course, but it seemed to be only a formality."

Bliss said "Ah!" noncommittally. He was trying to size her up. Whether or not she'd originally intended to meet someone, the fact remained that respectable girls didn't stick around by themselves till one in the morning at joints like the Queen of Hearts. And she certainly wasn't hooked on gambling, if her desultory play at the table was anything to go by. But she wasn't a common tart, either. She had poise and style. More like a top-flight courtesan. Looking for a tycoon, perhaps, but willing to pass a little time with a presentable younger man who seemed to have money to fling about . . . She was certainly attractive, one of the most attractive women he'd ever met—and he'd met plenty. Not what he'd come for, of course—no good, businesswise. A taker, not a giver. Not of cash, anyway. But a dream of a girl. Worth a detour.

She said, "What about you? Have you been here before?"

"Only once. I thought I'd look in again as I'd nothing special on tonight, but the truth is I've no great taste for gambling. I think it's a mug's game, especially in a place like this."

"The house always wins, I suppose?"

"You bet it does. No one can beat the odds for long —that's why they can afford such lavish appointments." Bliss shook his head sagely. "Not my line at all."

The girl's clear blue eyes surveyed him. "What *is* your line?" she asked.

"Work, do you mean? Oh, I dabble here and there. My passport says I'm a journalist."

"Then I suppose you are."

"In a modest, free-lance sort of way. I do occasional articles—travel experiences, oddities of the social scene, that kind of thing. Mostly for the Sundays. I even get paid for them."

"Very well paid, I should think, if you can afford to lose all that money at roulette without turning a hair."

"Oh, I have other resources. Anyway, I was showing off a bit tonight. Would you care for another drink?"

"Thank you."

Bliss ordered the same again. "And you—do *you* have a line?"

"I'm a beauty specialist," Corinne said.

Bliss smiled. "I should have known. Are you a free lance, too?"

She nodded. "I was with Wanda's in Piccadilly for a while, but I prefer having my own clients. It's so much pleasanter to be independent, don't you agree?"

"I do indeed." With a twinkle he added, "I imagine we see eye to eye about a lot of things."

"I wouldn't be at all surprised."

Bliss met her innocent blue gaze, and smiled again. They understood each other—there was really no more to be said. It had been a very efficient pickup, on both sides. A quick reconnaissance, a little gentle fencing, a significant remark or two—and no nonsense. Just how he liked it. Urbane, civilized . . . He finished his drink, glanced at his watch. "M'm—nearly two o'clock."

"Yes, it's time I was going." Corinne slid off her stool.

"Have you a car?" Bliss asked.

"No, I left mine at home. I was relying on my escort. It's all right—I'll get a taxi."

"I'd be happy to drive you, if you'd allow me."

"Well—it's very kind of you. I live in Knightsbridge. Is that much out of your way?"

"Where you live could never be out of my way," Bliss said. "My car's around the corner. I'll get it, and meet you in the foyer in ten minutes."

He walked around to the mews in a glow of expectation. Unless his antennae were deceiving him, this was going to be a night to remember. His pickup wasn't just a lovely piece of female flesh—there was something special about her, something that enormously excited him. Perhaps it was her cool reserve, her air of untouchability, that went so improbably with her behavior. The contrast between the way she acted and the way she looked. Angelically innocent in the dress —"white flower of a blameless life" and all that—or a bluebell in the snow, delicate and virginal. Bliss smiled at the extravagance of his fancies. All the same, there was something in it. A woman who looked pure and behaved earthy could be maddeningly stimulating.

He turned into the mews. It was empty of cars except for the Mercedes, which stood in deep shadow beside a wall. He unlocked the door and slid in behind the wheel. For a moment he sat in the dark car, feeling for his cigarette case. As he fumbled, another car pulled up in the street a few yards ahead of him, opposite the mews entrance. A man in the passenger seat wound down his window and stuck his head out. Bliss was about to flick on his lighter when, to his utter astonishment, the man tied something over the lower part of his face and poked the barrel of a gun out of the window. Immediately, the car roared away. There was a screech of tires as it took the corner, then a short burst of gunfire from the vicinity of the club and the crash of breaking glass. Someone screamed.

Bliss lit his dangling cigarette and drew deeply on it. Then he drove around to the front of the club. Everything there was in chaos. People were streaming out of the foyer, milling about in the street, talking in loud, excited voices. The commissionaire and several other men were bending over a prostrate form on the pavement. A trickle of blood was snaking into the gutter. Bliss left his car at the curb and pushed his way through the crowd to the shattered front door. As he passed the stricken man, he saw that it was the fat proprietor, Lou Savona.

Corinne was just coming into the foyer. She was wearing a full-length coat of sapphire mink and looked, Bliss thought, quite stunning.

"What's everyone rushing about for?" she asked. "What's happened?"

"Someone's shot the owner." Bliss took her arm and propelled her gently out of the club and past the throng on the pavement. "I wouldn't look if I were you —it's a bit gory." But she did look, and he felt her shudder as she saw the trail of blood.

By now the police were on the scene. A dark figure in a crash helmet was sorting out the traffic. Several others were questioning bystanders. Bliss guided Corinne through the jam of cars to the Mercedes and helped her in. "Sorry about that," he said, as he settled himself in the driver's seat. "Spoils a nice evening."

"It's horrible." Corinne was pale, and looked scared. "I *hate* the sight of blood."

"Well, I did warn you."

A helmeted figure appeared at the window. A police sergeant. "Excuse me, sir—did you happen to see anything?"

"Yes, they were in a black car, officer." It was professional instinct with Bliss, a part of his image-making, to help the police when he could; and his first response was automatic.

"Did you see the men, sir?" The sergeant's tone was eager.

Belatedly, Bliss realized where he was heading. Next thing he'd be having to give evidence. He backpedaled smartly. "Not really, sergeant. Just a glimpse."

"Where were you, sir?"

Bliss jerked his head. "Getting my car from the mews round the corner."

"I see." The sergeant took out his notebook. "I wonder if you'd mind letting me have your name and address?"

"Do I have to?"

"You don't have to, sir, but it might be useful."

"Then I'd sooner not, officer. Honestly, I can't help you. Goodnight." Bliss pressed the starter and drove quickly away.

There was a little silence in the car. Then Corinne said, "*Did* you see much?"

"Quite a bit, as a matter of fact." Bliss told her about the black car pulling up, and the man at the window, and the gun.

Corinne drew her coat more closely round her. "I'm terrified of violence."

"Who isn't?"

"Did you see his face?"

"Sure I saw it. But I don't fancy getting involved as a witness. They mess you about for weeks and they don't even say thank you. Now, where are we making for?"

"Everton Close, please. Just behind Harrods."

Bliss nodded. "I think I know it."

The journey was short and it passed mostly in silence. Bliss did try to chat a little at first, but Corinne was unresponsive and he soon gave up. As he set her down at her door she said, "I won't ask you in if you don't mind. I feel a bit shaken."

"That's all right." He'd already realized that the sizzling program he'd planned would have to be postponed. "There's always another day. What about having dinner with me tomorrow?"

"Well, yes—thank you. I'd like that."

"The Gourmet in Frith Street. Seven-thirty. Okay?"

"Okay," she said. "I'll look forward to it."

By the time Bliss got home and to bed the shooting incident was already fading from his mind. He slept soundly through what remained of the night and woke in the middle hours of the morning quite refreshed and in his customarily cheerful spirits. It was true he'd made no progress on the fortune-seeking front, but he felt sure something would occur to him before long and meanwhile he had a beckoning date, a prospect to dwell on pleasurably through the day. A little wine, a little food, a little dalliance with a whizzbang of a girl. What more could anyone ask?

He had just finished dressing when there was a ring at the bell. He went unhurriedly to the door and opened it. Two men stood on the landing, both strangers to him. One was stocky and solid-looking, the other tall and lanky. Bliss guessed they were policemen by their stance, authoritative, yet faintly defensive. As a lawbreaker who'd got away with it, he had a certain sympathy with policemen. Decent chaps on the whole, but rarely up to their job. Doggedly pressing on with their duties, but not exactly bright. Pushed around by the public, fair game for criticism, always having to watch their step.

"Good morning, sir," the stocky one said. "Mr. Bliss, isn't it?" He was a man in his early thirties, darkly handsome, with a penetrating gaze that Bliss felt he must have practiced.

"That's right," Bliss said.

"My name's Kirby, sir—Detective Inspector Kirby. This is Detective Sergeant Groves. I believe you're the owner of the gray Mercedes car that's parked outside the house."

"I am," Bliss said. "What's the trouble? Dirty number plates?"

The inspector gave a perfunctory smile. "I understand you were in the vicinity of the Queen of Hearts Club when a man was shot last night."

"Oh—*that's* it." Bliss had rather thought it must be. He'd committed no indiscretions that he could remember in the recent past, made no mistakes, so there was no other reason why the police should call on him. All the same, their visit surprised him. "How did you get on to me?" he asked.

"The officer who spoke to you made a note of your car number," Kirby said, in a tone of slight reproof.

"I see." Bliss did some fast thinking. The police were obviously going to work hard on him over the shooting, and they wouldn't take kindly to stalling. So he'd better appear forthcoming. But he needn't involve himself. It was just a matter of handling their questions skillfully. Cooperation without information—that was the line. The regretful good citizen . . . "Well," he said, "I doubt if I can tell you anything more than I told the sergeant. If I'd thought I could help I'd have given him my address at the time. Still, come in."

"Thank you, sir—we won't keep you long." The two policemen followed Bliss into the sitting room.

"What happened to the man who was shot?" Bliss asked. "Is he dead?"

Kirby, whose eyes had been flicking around the room, brought his glance sharply back to focus on Bliss. "No, he was lucky, sir. So were several other people, considering that the front of the building was sprayed with a submachine gun. It could have been a massacre. A bullet went through his chest but missed everything vital. He'll recover."

"What was he doing out there on the pavement, anyway?"

"It seems someone rang him up with a bogus message, sir. Told him the police were out in front and would be grateful if he'd go and speak to them. So he went, and was shot down at the club door by the man in the car. Nice timing. I imagine someone must have given the driver a signal."

Bliss tut-tutted. "Shocking affair! And you've no idea who might have done it?"

"We've a few thoughts about it," Kirby said. "Nothing you could call evidence. Between ourselves, this fellow Savona is a pretty unsavory character. We've had our eyes on him for some time. Again, we've no proof, but we think he's concerned in several unpleasant rackets. The gunman could have been one of his rivals—he's had gang trouble before." Kirby's manner grew brisker. "Now, sir, I'd be much obliged if you'd tell me exactly what you saw."

Bliss's brows drew together in a little frown of concentration. "Well—I was sitting in my car in Angel Mews without lights, feeling for a cigarette, and this black car pulled up. A man wound down the window and looked out but I didn't pay any particular attention to him—not till he suddenly covered the lower part of his face and pushed the gun out. I was pretty shaken then, I can tell you, especially as the gun seemed to be pointing at me. But it wasn't, and the car moved off, and that was that. The whole thing was over in a moment."

"All the same," Kirby said, "you did see the man's face before he covered up?"

"I saw it, yes—but only for a matter of seconds."

"Could you describe it?"

Bliss's frown deepened. "How do you describe a face that you've only seen for a couple of seconds? There was nothing special about it—nothing to remember. It was just—a face."

"Surely it must have left some impression on your mind, sir?"

Bliss shook his head. "Not really. Not one that I can put into words, anyway. I'd only mislead you if I tried."

"Would you recognize the face if you saw it again?"

Bliss pondered. "I have absolutely no idea. I might, I suppose—though I very much doubt it."

"H'm. What did the gunman cover his face with? A scarf? A handkerchief?"

"Not a handkerchief. It was something blue, I think. Dark, anyway. It could have been a scarf—but it all happened so fast I can't be sure."

"What about the driver of the car?"

"I didn't see him at all. The other man was in the way."

"Have you any idea what make of car it was?"

Again, Bliss shook his head. "I only saw it sideways on. It was a black saloon, fairly big, quite an ordinary car. It could have been any popular model."

Kirby grunted. "Yes—well, we're not getting very far, are we?"

"I'm afraid not," Bliss said, with every appearance of regret. "I'm sorry I can't be of more use. Look, there

must have been other people around. Can't anyone
else help you?"

"If they can, they won't," Kirby said. "It's always the
same with these gang fights. Witnesses melt away."

Bliss nodded thoughtfully. "I can't say I altogether
blame them. I'm no hero, either. Quite frankly, if I
knew I'd helped to shop one of these types I'd want
to put a whole continent between me and his friends
before I felt safe."

Kirby smiled, a thin, sardonic smile. "I expect we
could arrange that, sir. We'd fix you up in Timbuctu
if it would help us to get our man."

Bliss laughed. "It's a nice thought, Inspector, but
you won't have to go to that trouble in my case. With
the best will in the world, I can't tell you any more
than I have."

"I see, sir. All right, we'll leave it at that for the
moment, though I'll probably be getting in touch with
you again. Thank you for giving us your time." Kirby
picked up his hat, gave a final, slightly disgruntled
glance around the room, and departed with the sergeant.

Bliss slowed the car at the Hyde Park Corner
roundabout and said, as though the thought had just
occurred to him, "What about dropping in at my place
for a last drink?"

"That sounds quite a pleasant idea." Corinne had
completely recovered from the shock of the previous
night. She was sitting back in the passenger seat of
the Mercedes, snug in mink, looking very relaxed and
obviously enjoying the smooth, effortless ride.

Bliss was feeling pretty pleased with life, too. Dinner at the Gourmet had been a great success. A maître d'hôtel who'd welcomed him as an old friend. Favorite corner table. Discreet lighting. Attentive waiters. Splendid food and wine. Everything to impress. And a girl who'd seemed more alluring every time he'd looked at her. Almost no serious talk—just a word or two about the shooting and about Bliss's stalling efforts with the police, amusingly recounted. Plenty of light banter. Lots of laughs. Sexy overtones. Just the ticket . . . Now, with caviar, a steak *au poivre* and half a bottle of excellent Chambertin under his belt, he felt mellow and in the mood for love.

They reached Hampstead in less than twenty minutes. Bampton Gardens, always a pleasant road, looked particularly attractive in the car's bright headlights. Its flowering shrubs and magnolia and bright green chestnut shoots showed up vividly, while its Victorian turrets and cupolas and oriel windows were well lost in the darkness above. Bliss parked behind a neighbor's ancient Bentley and led the way in to number 15. "No lift here," he said. "Good for the figure. No porter either. Good for the reputation."

Corinne laughed. "That's thoughtful of you." She gazed around the spacious lobby. "It's quite imposing, isn't it, in a solid sort of way? All this mahogany . . . Oughtn't you to be wearing a chain of office?"

"I'm against chains of any sort," Bliss said, with a grin. He picked up his evening paper from the table and they climbed the stairs to the flat.

In the hall, he took Corinne's coat. She looked like a million dollars with it on, but he preferred her without it. She was wearing a slinky dress of dark blue silk that drew attention to her best points. A pretty nice parcel, Bliss thought, which he'd take great pleasure in unwrapping further. "Make yourself at home," he said. "What would you like to drink—brandy?"

"May I look around first? I love seeing other people's flats."

"Sure—we'll do a conducted tour." Bliss began to show her the rooms. "Here you are. Kitchen, where I boil my morning egg . . . Bathroom and usual offices . . . Bedroom for sleeping, *et al.* . . . Sitting room with view . . . Small bar in alcove—I had that put in for fun. . . . Study, with large cupboard under rafters, opening off."

"M'm—you do yourself well, don't you?" Corinne was obviously impressed. Bliss could almost hear her making her mental notes, like a taximeter ticking up shillings. The furniture, the curtains, the carpets, the pictures, the concealed lighting. Practically valuing the place. Not that he minded. He'd looked *her* over pretty hard, come to that.

She peered inside the cupboard. It was as large as a small room. Bliss switched on the light for her. "My glory hole," he said.

She nodded. "Very useful." There were several piles of old paperbacks stacked on the floor, three or four suitcases, some pairs of discarded shoes, tools, bits of photographic apparatus, and various unidentifiable bundles. Corinne fingered the carved top of an enormous oak chest. It was black with age and had a badly split lid. "This could be quite nice, couldn't it? Why don't you have it done up?"

"I've never got around to it," Bliss said. "The last tenants left it behind, so I shouldn't think it amounts to much. Full of worm, I wouldn't be surprised. Well, there you are—that's about the lot."

"I like your pad," Corinne said.

They went back into the hall. Corinne looked around, as though she had lost her bearings. Bliss slipped his hands under her arms and over her breasts from behind, and kissed the back of her neck.

She half turned her head, smiling. "Well?" she said.

"Well what?"

She had her bearings now. She was looking at the open bedroom door. "What are we waiting for?"

Bliss stirred, got out of bed, fetched his cigarette case, returned to the bed and stood gazing down at Corinne with a relaxed smile. He still thought she looked wonderful, and in several new ways she'd proved she was. He couldn't imagine himself tiring of her, not for some time, anyway. He had absolutely no romantic feelings about her, no illusions. In his mind he had her pretty well summed up now. She was attractive, carnal, unscrupulous and mercenary. In fact, the female counterpart of himself. It was a case of like calling to like. Loud and clear.

He lit two cigarettes and gave her one. "Well, that was quite an experience," he said. "Men have died for less! We must see more of each other."

"You can hardly see more of me than you are doing," Corinne said. Though she was reclining naked on the bed of a man she'd met only twenty-four hours before, having enjoyed herself in a manner to which she was obviously well accustomed, she still somehow contrived to look both innocent and surprised. Her eyes were bigger and bluer than ever. It was, Bliss thought, quite an act.

He began to dress. "Would you still like that brandy?"

"I'd rather have coffee, if you don't mind."

"Okay, I'll make it. No need for you to move—you go nicely with the decor. Here, have the paper." He gave her the *Evening Standard* and went into the kitchen.

He was back in a few minutes with a tray, a jug and cups. "I make coffee the straight way," he said. "No percolator nonsense. Would you like it black?"

"Please."

"Sugar?"

"Two, please."

"Anything in the headlines?"

"I was just reading about a man who stole two million pounds . . . Max Banda."

"Oh, that fellow."

"You know about him, do you?"

"Sure. He used to run a financial empire and a seraglio of lovely girls. He lost the empire, so now I suppose he's lost the girls too. What's happened to him?"

"He's been sent for trial."

"I'm not surprised."

"It says the police opposed bail, but the court allowed it."

"Really? I bet the police are mad about that. Now they'll have to keep an eye on him."

Corinne put the paper down. "Two million's a nice round sum, isn't it? I wonder what he did with it."

"Stashed it away, I should think. Not that it'll do him much good now. What a clot!"

"Why do you say that?"

"Because he is. What's the good of being a financial wizard if you haven't got the sense to keep out of jail? I've read quite a bit about Banda—he's a brilliant fellow, computer mind, Midas touch—all that stuff. Yet what did he do? When things got sticky, he forged documents. Financial documents involving huge sums, that were bound to come under scrutiny. An absolutely sure-fire way of getting into the pokey. Of course he was caught. He hadn't a hope."

"You sound quite worked up about it."

"Well, I hate incompetence. If a chap sets out to swindle, he should do it efficiently. There are too many bunglers in this world."

Corinne laughed softly. *"You're* not a bungler, anyway. I can vouch for that."

It was nearly one in the morning by the time Bliss had driven Corinne home and returned to Hampstead. He got himself a small nightcap of whiskey and settled down for a few minutes with the paper Corinne had been reading.

His attention was held by the big headline about the erring tycoon, and he read the story through. It ran:

Mr. Max Banda, the fifty-year-old City financier, was today committed for trial at the Old Bailey by the West London magistrate on charges of misappropriation and forgery involving sums of nearly two million pounds. Banda reserved his defense.

Defending counsel, Mr. R. G. Frew, Q.C., asking

for bail, said it was unlikely the Old Bailey hearing could take place before May, or possibly even June, owing to the complexity of the matters at issue. In such cases, bail was customary. Counsel also maintained that the preparation of his client's defense would be seriously handicapped if he were detained in prison. Opposing bail, Chief Superintendent Harris, of the Fraud Squad, said that in view of the gravity of the charges it was feared that Banda might attempt to leave the country. Bail was granted in two sureties of £65,000 on condition that Banda surrender his passport.

Below the story there was a single-column picture captioned, "Mr. Max Banda arriving at his Sussex home after the hearing." It showed a thickset man getting out of a taxi, holding a newspaper in front of his face to shield it from the camera.

It was while Bliss was looking at the picture that, in its simplest form, the idea came to him.

Humming softly to himself, "Summer Suns Are Glowing," he went into the study and took down *Who's Who in the City,* a work of reference that he'd found of outstanding value professionally. As he'd supposed, Banda rated a long entry. Born London, 1918. Son of Oscar Banda and Martha Holtz. Educated Heidelberg, Cambridge. Chairman of . . . Bliss ran through the list. There were nearly twenty companies —banks, finance houses, industrial concerns—all well known and respected until the crash a few months before. Publications—all financial or technical. Recreations—golf and chess. No mention of any marriage. Address—Lowndes Court, W.1 and Downside, Lushington, Sussex.

Bliss looked up Lushington in a gazetteer. It was a

village in the South Downs, a few miles from Lewes. He stood for a moment, brows drawn together. Then he opened the door of the glory hole and switched on the light. Afterward, he sat thinking.

Looked at *in vacuo,* his idea was, of course, preposterous. No sane man would entertain it for a moment. It was too ambitious, too risky—and probably quite impracticable. In any other circumstances, he'd have rejected it out of hand.

But in the special circumstances that existed—that was another matter. . . . The gunman at the Queen of Hearts. The chivying by Inspector Kirby. The talk of Timbuctu . . . Bliss chuckled at the notion. The irony would be delicious, if he could swing it. And it wasn't impossible, considering what he had to offer. A quid for a quo, that's what it would be. Quite a few quid, in fact! Of course, he'd have to go on appearing reluctant. Give way slowly under pressure. Not take any initiative himself. With luck, he wouldn't need to. Kirby had said he would be in touch again.

Bliss's thoughts ranged widely over the fantastic problems and difficulties. At this stage he hadn't a clue how he'd get over them, but he could see it would be tremendous fun trying. He'd wanted something challenging, something to surmount—and this would be an Everest. It would need nerve, foresight, meticulous planning, daring action.

Action . . . Now that would be one of the problems. There'd be too much action for one man working alone —and Bliss had always preferred to work alone. This idea would require at least one reliable partner, someone with a head as cool as his own. Which practically ruled it out. He knew no one who qualified, no one he could wholly trust.

Suddenly he thought of Corinne. She was cool enough. A real tough baby, if ever there was one. Shrewd, calculating, self-reliant, sharply intelligent. Not so cool when it came to violence, perhaps—but there was no element of violence in his idea. Only cunning, subterfuge, pretense—and he was quite sure Corinne could put on an act with anyone. From what he'd seen of her, she'd make an excellent co-plotter, and she'd be just as useful as a man in taking a share of the weight off him. More useful, in some situations. It was certainly a thought. . . . Of course, she might not want to do it, but it would be worth sounding her out, if things ever got that far.

Anyway, he'd sleep on his idea. Let it mature a bit. See what happened.

What happened was that there was a telephone call from Inspector Kirby before Bliss had finished shaving next morning, and before he'd had time to consider his plan any further. The inspector's tone was urgent. "I'm sorry to trouble you so early, Mr. Bliss, but this is important. We've detained a man on suspicion of the Queen of Hearts shooting. Now could you possibly attend an identification parade at Gerald Street police station this morning, and see if you can pick out your gunman?"

"Well . . . ," Bliss began, and paused. He'd envisaged a much slower process than this—a gradual piecing together by him of the man's facial appearance, under police pressure and by an apparently superhuman effort of recollection, followed in due course by an arrest which would give him the opportunity he needed. Now, that had all been telescoped; fate was obviously hurrying him along. Not that it mattered— he'd already worked out what his attitude must be. One of reluctant cooperation . . .

"Do you think it would do any good?" he said. "As I told you, I barely saw the fellow. I don't suppose for a moment I'll be able to pick him out."

"You never know, sir. You did agree there was just a chance you might recognize him if you saw him again."

True, Bliss thought. A good thing, now, that he hadn't been too definite. "Well," he said, "it's a very slim chance."

"All the same, sir, I'd be grateful if you'd try. It won't take up much of your time—not more than an hour, I'd say, including the journey. I do urge you to cooperate with us."

"I'd like to do that, of course," Bliss said, and paused again. The time seemed to have come to strike the first note of personal disquiet. "I must say I'm not too keen on getting involved with these characters."

"Just taking a look down the line won't involve you, sir. No one will know who you are."

"Not if I don't recognize anyone," Bliss said. "But suppose I do. What then?"

"I suggest we deal with that situation if and when it arises, sir. You don't seem to think it will. There's no point in crossing bridges before we come to them."

"Could I wear dark glasses?"

"Well, I wouldn't recommend that, if you're trying to identify somebody. But there's no reason why your face shouldn't be partly covered, if it would make you feel happier."

"It certainly would," Bliss said. "All right, Inspector. I doubt very much whether I shall be able to help you, but I'll take a look. When would you like me to come?"

"I'd suggest eleven o'clock, sir, if that's convenient for you. Sharp, if you can manage it. We have to bring people in out of the street and they don't like to be kept waiting."

"Very well," Bliss said. "I'll be there."

Eleven o'clock was just striking as he entered Gerald Street police station. He gave his name to the desk sergeant, and Kirby appeared almost at once. The inspector greeted Bliss cordially.

"Very good of you to come, sir. I do appreciate it. I hope it hasn't interfered too much with your work."

"As it happens, not at all," Bliss said. "I'm a free-lance journalist, so my time's my own."

"Ah—that's fortunate. Well, we're all ready for you."

"What do I have to do, Inspector?"

"It's very simple. Just walk down the line at your own pace and take a look at each man. Don't say anything. If you think you recognize the gunman, put your hand on his arm. That's all."

Bliss nodded. "What about covering my face?"

"I've a clean handkerchief here, if that's all right with you." Kirby stepped behind him and tied the handkerchief so that it hung like a veil over his nose and mouth. "How's that, sir?"

Bliss made a slight adjustment. "Seems okay."

"Then if you'd follow me . . ." Kirby led the way out through a back door and into a yard. Ten or a dozen men were lined up against a high brick wall as though awaiting a firing squad. They were all about the same

height, all about the same age, all—at a distance—re-
markably alike. A sergeant and several constables were
standing by.

Bliss began to move slowly along the line. This new
role of his wasn't too easy a one, under watchful eyes.
He hadn't much doubt he'd know the gunman again,
but after what he'd said to Kirby, he mustn't be too
hesitant, or the identification would lose some of its
value as evidence. And he must remember that he was
supposed to be nervous. As he moved forward, he kept
well out of reach of the men he was inspecting.

He was halfway along the line now. Of course, it
was quite possible that the gunman wasn't there at all
—the police being notorious bunglers. It would be just
like them to have picked up the wrong bloke.

Suddenly he stopped.

The man he was looking at was heavily built, with
shoulders and biceps that bulged under his jacket. He
had crisp curly hair, sandy in color, with a pronounced
widow's peak. His cheekbones curved outward, and his
ears were large. He had pale, dead-fish eyes.

Bliss looked at the man for about three seconds.
Then he stretched out a hand and touched him on the
arm.

Back in the station Kirby removed the handkerchief
from Bliss's face and conducted him into an inner office. He was jubilant at the result of the parade. "So it
wasn't a waste of time after all," he said, pulling out a
chair for Bliss and taking a seat himself. "You picked
your man—and he turns out to be our man, too. Well
done, sir."

"It's extraordinary," Bliss said. "I really didn't think

I'd know him again, but when I saw those features it somehow all came back. Just shows how wrong one can be." He ran the back of his hand across his forehead, as though wiping away a little sweat. His forehead wasn't damp, but he thought it unlikely that Kirby could see it wasn't, across the table. "Who is he, Inspector? He looks a very ugly customer at close quarters."

"He is," Kirby said. "One of the worst. His name's Jack Olsen and he runs a chain of clubs in Soho. He's been at odds with Lou Savona for quite a while. They've had several nasty fights. That's why we pulled him in for questioning. We've never been able to nail him before, but now, with your help, we should be able to put him away for years."

Bliss's disciplined features registered disquiet. "Now wait a minute, Inspector. I agreed to come here because you pressed me—and of course, as things have turned out, you were right to do so. But I don't want to get in any deeper than I am."

"I'm afraid that's unavoidable now, sir."

"You mean you'll want me to give evidence that I saw him?"

"You're the only one who can," Kirby said.

"Well, I don't know. . . ." Bliss frowned. "Swearing in court that you've seen a man is a bit different from just thinking you have. After all, Olsen *looks* like a crook—I could have been misled by that, I suppose. I could have been mistaken."

Kirby smiled indulgently. He was used to timid witnesses trying to backtrack. "You weren't mistaken, sir. I happen to know that Olsen was the gunman."

"How do you know?"

"Because when we started to question him about his movements on the night of the shooting he gave a false alibi. He's got a place on an island in the Thames, near Maidenhead. He said that on the evening in question he drove down there with three friends and was playing poker with them until four in the morning. The friends say he was, too."

"It sounds quite an alibi to me," Bliss said.

"That's because you don't know his friends, sir. They were all lying in their teeth—and by a stroke of luck I was able to prove it."

"Really? How?"

"I went down there myself yesterday to take a look around. Olsen has had the house fitted up with a lot of expensive gadgets, the way these gangsters do. One of them is a bar across the causeway that leads to the island. It works electronically. When a car approaches, the bar lifts and a bell rings in the house. It lifted for me. I was just going through when I saw a bird fly out of the end of the bar—the end that was pointing toward the ground when the bar was raised. That set me thinking, and I stopped to take a closer look. The bar is hollow, and there was a nest in the end of it. A robin's nest, I'm told. There were three eggs, and two of them had fallen out and smashed on the ground when the bar went up. Most of the nest had come out, too. If Olsen and his cronies had gone through the night before, it would have happened then."

Bliss looked at the inspector with genuine admiration. Here, at least, was no bungler. In his field, Kirby was evidently an operator of Bliss's own caliber. A worthy opponent. A man it would be a pleasure to outwit.

"Well, I call that brilliant," he said. "Real Hawkeye stuff. I shouldn't think one policeman in a hundred would have been so observant."

"I wouldn't say that, sir. In our line of business we're trained to watch for the smallest details. Anyhow, as you can see, the alibi's broken. And a man who offers a false alibi stands half convicted."

"In that case," Bliss said, "surely you don't need me."

"Oh, yes, we do, Mr. Bliss. We need you for the other half—the most important half. Someone has to say he saw Olsen near the scene of the shooting, with a gun. If we don't have that we can't even bring a charge. Giving a false alibi doesn't by itself prove he shot Savona—it only proves he had something to hide. He could admit that he lied, and say he was trying to conceal something else. He wouldn't even need to say what. No, it's the two halves together that clinch the case. That's why we need your evidence."

"I see." Bliss took up the threads of his act. "Well, I must say I never expected to get mixed up in a thing like this. I don't like it at all." He stared glumly at the floor. "The humiliating fact is, Inspector, that now I'm actually faced with the prospect of giving evidence against a man like Olsen I'm no different from those witnesses you mentioned who melted away."

"Except that *you* can't melt away," Kirby said.

"You mean that if I tried to, I'd be subpoenaed?"

"I would think almost certainly, sir, though it's rarely a satisfactory procedure. A witness who gives his evidence under threat of a penalty often feels resentful and speaks without interest or conviction. A horse to the water, you know . . . That's why I'd infinitely pre-

fer you to testify of your own free will. After all, Mr.
Bliss, it *is* your duty as a citizen."

"I realize that," Bliss said unhappily. "And I've always considered myself a pretty good citizen. I believe
in law and order. I believe people should help the
police."

"Well, sir, now's the time to put your beliefs into
practice. This man Olsen is a menace to society. He's
involved with drugs, protection, women—every racket
you can think of. He runs around with a gang of thugs
and behaves as though he's above the law. This is the
first time we've had a chance to pin anything on him,
and with your help we can finish him for good."

"I dare say," Bliss said gloomily. "What worries me
is that his friends may finish *me* for good! I wouldn't
be the first witness to end up in the gutter with his
head kicked in. . . . I suppose I couldn't give my evidence anonymously?"

Kirby looked doubtful. "Courts do sometimes
make special arrangements about withholding names,
though in your case I doubt if it would help. Olsen's
gang could easily find out who you were if they wanted
to. They've probably got contacts at the Queen of
Hearts, and you're a member there. Your name and
address are on record. But you needn't have any anxiety, Mr. Bliss. If you're really concerned about your
safety, we'll give you protection."

"For how long, Inspector?"

"For as long as you feel you need it."

"From what I've read," Bliss said, "men like Olsen
and his friends have pretty long memories. I might
need it for ten years. Or longer. Could you guarantee
my safety for ten years?"

"Well, I don't know about that, sir. But I think your fears are exaggerated. These gangsters operate in a world of their own and they don't often step outside it. They're ready enough to take revenge on their own kind, particularly informers, but it's very rare for them to attack an outside witness, an ordinary member of the public."

Bliss looked far from convinced. "It may be rare, Inspector, but it's not a thing one wants to take chances with, is it? I'd always feel there was a threat hanging over me. And there's something else—I'm not the only person involved. I'm planning to get married, and I certainly wouldn't want my fiancée to get caught up in a squalid business like this—perhaps even having to share the danger. It wouldn't be fair to her. Frankly, I just don't know what to say."

Kirby pushed back his chair. "Well, Mr. Bliss, you don't have to make up your mind today. I realize it's not an easy decision for you. Why not talk to your fiancée about it—put the whole position before her and see what she thinks?"

Bliss nodded. "Yes, I'll do that." He gave Kirby a final troubled glance. "Believe me, Inspector, I'd like to help, if only I could see a safe way of doing it. I'm as anxious to see this thug jailed as you are. I'd even take reasonable risks, but . . ." He broke off. "Anyway, I'll talk to Corinne about it and let you know."

Bliss drove back to Hampstead in splendid spirits. With almost no effort on his part, the plan which yesterday had seemed so crude and embryonic was beginning to take shape very nicely. The interview itself had been a bit of a drag—all that long-winded waffling

about danger couldn't have been more alien to his nature—but the right foundations had been laid and he'd
established a relationship with Kirby which he could
now start to exploit. Yes, on the whole things were going very well indeed!

Of course, if he did give evidence against Olsen he'd
be stepping into a pretty exposed position. The defense
would no doubt scrutinize him closely. They might
even try to dig up something to his discredit, maybe
employ somebody to nose around among his private
affairs. But he'd already thought about that aspect of
the matter and decided there was little to fear. For
three years he'd been living the life of a respectable
citizen of means, and the name of Michael Bliss was in
the clear. All his earlier ploys had been carried out
under various aliases, so the Bliss name would bring
back no dangerous memories to anyone when it appeared in the papers. There were no old photographs
of him scattered around, to be picked up by an enter-
prising investigator. He'd always been most careful
about that. And the press would have no chance to
take any new pictures, if he went to court under a close
police guard. Short of actually running into one of his
former victims, his past was safely buried.

Right. So now for the next move. The recruitment of
his partner!

Corrine disposed herself decoratively on Bliss's sofa.
"What's it all about, Mike?" She had just arrived at
Bampton Gardens in her blue Mini car, after a telephone call from Bliss that had been urgent in tone but
vague in content.

Bliss surveyed her, conscious of stirrings that had

nothing to do with his plan. "Extraordinary how you always manage to look so seductive," he said.

"There's no need to make it sound such an effort! Come on—tell!"

Bliss switched his mind back to business. "Well—it's about money."

"Oh, good! That's always interesting."

"How would you like to make some? A great deal, in fact?"

Corinne smiled. "What a silly thing to ask!"

"It's not as silly as it sounds," Bliss said. "The method, though lucrative, would not be legal."

"Oh . . ." Corinne met the challenge of his gaze with limpid eyes. "Well, I can't say I'm particularly surprised—I've been wondering about you since we met. What really *is* your line?"

"As I told you, I dabble. Go anywhere, do anything, can drive car. Mostly, I'm what you'd call a con man. A highly successful one, I may say, though at the moment I'm getting a bit low on funds. There you are—cards on the table!"

There was a little pause. Then Corinne said, "Well, I'm not too terribly fussy."

"You've no objection to a bit of illegality?"

"Not in principle. Not as long as I don't get caught."

"If I thought either of us would get caught I wouldn't suggest it. Before I tell you any more, though, I'll have to ask you one or two questions. They're a bit personal, but I hope you won't mind—after all, *I've* come clean. I'm just trying to avoid trouble later on by getting a few basic things clear now."

"I wish you'd stop being so mysterious," Corinne said. "What are the questions?"

"We'll start with an easy one. Was that really your first visit to the Queen of Hearts?"

"It was."

"Are you known around gambling joints?"

"I've never been near one before. That was just an experiment." Corinne's eyes twinkled. "Ocean liners are more my mark."

"Very sensible. Safer, and more comfortable. Have you a police record?"

Corinne shook her head. "Not so far, dear."

"Any trouble with the police at all?"

"None at all."

"Good. The same goes for me. So as far as the world's concerned, your character's unblemished?"

"Absolutely spotless."

"That's what I hoped to hear. . . . Now how about debts? Do you owe much?"

"Nothing to speak of. I'm solvent, if that's what you mean. Just about."

"No angry creditors at your heels?"

"No."

"What about your recent boy friends? Anyone with a claim on you? Anyone who's likely to chase you up?"

"Not at the moment."

"That fellow who flew to Los Angeles . . . ?"

"I'm afraid I invented him."

"H'm—I guessed you might have. . . . And the man who gave you that diamond?"

"He died."

Bliss's eyebrows went up. "Natural causes, I hope?"

"Oh, yes. He was *very* old."

"I suppose you wore him out, lucky devil! Now, where was I? Oh, yes . . . What about your clients?"

"My clients?"

"Yes—your beauty business."

"Oh—*that!*" Corinne laughed. "I expect I see about as many clients as you write newspaper articles."

"You mean it's your cover story?"

"You could call it that."

"Fair enough—I just wondered. Any relatives keeping tabs on you?"

"Don't be dreary. I shed them all long ago."

"I did the same. Your passport's in order, I suppose?"

"Of course."

"How's your French?"

"Not at all bad, actually. I once knew a Frenchman."

Bliss grinned. "I bet your other languages are good, too! Well, that's the end of the catechism, and you're through with flying colors. Ten out of ten."

"Thank you, sir."

"So now I'll tell you my idea. . . ."

"After that buildup, it ought to be really something."

"It is," Bliss said. "If it comes off, it'll be a short cut to riches for both of us."

"I could do with a drink," Corinne said. "I feel a bit overwhelmed." Fifteen minutes had passed, fifteen minutes of lucid and orderly exposition by the maestro and of fascinated listening by the pupil. Now the flow had stopped.

Bliss went to the bar, mixed two weak gins and French, and brought them back. "That was only an outline, of course. I'm still pressing on with the details." He gave Corinne her glass. "Well, what do you think?"

"The way you put it," Corinne said, "it sounds fabulous. But . . ."

"But what?"

"It's so fabulous, I can't believe it'll work."

"It'll work if we get the go-ahead. I'm sure of it."

She regarded him quizzically. "You *are* sure, aren't you? I've never met a man with so much confidence in himself."

Bliss laughed. "If I hadn't confidence in myself, how could I expect others to trust me?"

"You must have been proved wrong sometimes."

"Oh, sure—but professionally not very often. Mostly I've been right, and over a pretty wide field. This plan breaks new ground, I know, but there's nothing in it I don't feel capable of carrying out, with your help."

"What would I have to do?"

"Well, drive quite a bit. There'd be a great deal of to-ing and fro-ing and the logistics would be impossible for one person on his own. Use your feminine charm to make the initial contact. Help me put on a convincing show with Kirby. Run some of the errands. Nothing very strenuous."

"There'd be quite big risks, though, wouldn't there?"

"There would be risks, of course, but reasonable ones, considering what we'd stand to gain. Almost none in the early stages. We'd merely be seeing how the land lay. The end could be a bit fraught, but if we weren't satisfied with the way things were going we could always pack it in."

Corinne nodded. "It would mean quite an upheaval for both of us, assuming it went through."

"Well, we're neither of us rooted to any particular spot. Personally, I'd welcome a change of domicile."

"I can't say I'd mind, either. How would we divide the money?"

"Oh, fifty-fifty, obviously."

"I only wondered." Corinne was silent for a while, ruminating. Presently she said, "What was that man like—the one you picked out at the identification parade?"

"Jack Olsen? Horrible. Looked a brute."

"Don't you think you're taking him a bit too lightly? Him and his friends?"

"I don't think so. I'm sure Kirby's right about these jokers—they'll carve each other up without a qualm but they don't usually operate outside their own circle. They're not keen on tangling with respectable people."

"I seem to remember reading about a case not long ago—some gang put a bomb in a car and it blew up when the engine started. I'm sure the man who was blown up wasn't one of the gang, and I believe he *was* a witness."

"I don't remember that. Anyway, it must have been exceptional."

"You could be exceptional too," Corinne said.

Bliss grinned. "You sound just like me talking to Kirby! Honestly, I don't believe there's much danger from the gang. Certainly none at all until the committal proceedings, because they won't know I'm in the picture till I've given my evidence. After that I'll make sure I keep out of their way."

"*I'd* certainly want to make sure," Corinne said. "I'm scared stiff at the thought of them."

"That's fine. You'll do a better line with the inspector if you're really scared. In point of fact, though, you won't be involved at all. You won't come to the court, your name won't be mentioned. As far as the gang's concerned, you can keep right out of it."

"Just so long as that's understood," Corinne said. "I don't mind taking a few risks with the police, but I don't want my face slashed."

"It's understood, Corinne—cross my heart! You'll stay in the background. . . . So what's your decision about the plan?"

"Well, the thought of all that money is rather tempting, isn't it? I'm probably crazy, but I think I'll take a chance and go along with you."

"That's my girl!" Bliss said. "I'm sure you won't regret it." He rubbed his hands together in lively expectation. "Right—now for the next round with old Hawkeye!"

At five o'clock that afternoon Bliss rang Scotland Yard. Inspector Kirby was out, but Bliss left a message asking if he would care to come to Hampstead for a talk that evening. At six Kirby rang back to say he was on his way, and at six-thirty he arrived. Bliss offered him a glass of dry sherry which, after a moment's hesitation, he accepted.

"Well," Bliss said, when they were comfortably seated, "I did as you suggested and talked the whole thing over with Corinne. I'm sorry you couldn't meet her, but she had a date this evening. I think you'd have approved of her attitude."

"Oh, yes?" Kirby's face brightened, and he drank a little sherry.

"She's scared, mind you—even more scared than I am, and that's saying something. She has an absolute horror of violence, and when I described Olsen and told her what sort of man he was, she was appalled. I said you'd offered me protection, but she felt the same way as I did about that—it's better than nothing, but not much of a guarantee in the long run. At the same time, she did say that if everyone ducked their responsibilities the thugs would soon be out on top, which would be terrible. And then she suddenly came up with an idea."

"Yes?" Kirby said again.

"The thing is, Corinne has always wanted to live in France after we're married. In Provence, to be exact —she's very romantic about that part of the world. Personally I don't much mind where I live as long as it's with her, though I must say I rather go for the warm weather and the wine. Anyway, we'd already discussed the possibility before this business came up, and as far as I'm concerned it's quite feasible. I've private means, as you've probably realized, and the articles I do as a free-lance journalist can be written anywhere. So, quite briefly, Corinne's idea is that I should give evidence at Olsen's trial, and that we should then go straight off to France without leaving any tracks. In that way, we'd be quite safe. Does that make sense to you?"

Kirby beamed. "It makes a great deal of sense, Mr. Bliss. If you're in a position to do that, and you'd like to do it, I'd say it was an ideal solution."

"That's what I thought. I know it seems a bit like running away, but at least I'd have done my civic duty first. Of course, I'd still need your protection at the time of the committal proceedings."

"That's understood, sir."

"And at the trial, too. In between, I think I'd go off to some quiet hotel in the country and lie low under a different name. Wouldn't that be the best thing?"

"It would probably save you anxiety, sir, and it would certainly save us trouble. It's what I'd have suggested myself."

"Good. Corinne probably wouldn't mind joining me there, either. She's anxious to keep right out of the picture while the hearings are on—she really is very frightened—and I'm determined she shall. That's my overriding interest, her safety and her peace of mind. Frankly, if I thought there was the slightest risk to her, now or later, wild horses wouldn't make me say I saw Olsen."

"I understand," Kirby said.

"Of course, we'll need a lot of help—with transport, tickets, preparations—that sort of thing. I wouldn't want anyone to get the notion I was leaving the country—in case I was being watched, and the trail was picked up. And I'd want a quick exit for the same reason, no hanging about at ports. Would you undertake to make all necessary arrangements for me, so that speed and secrecy were guaranteed?"

Kirby gave an emphatic nod. "If you'll give your evidence, Mr. Bliss, I'll be only too happy to fall in with any reasonable requests you care to make. I'll cooperate all along the line."

There was a little silence. Then Bliss said, "Very well, Inspector. It's a deal."

II

FROM A ROUGH wooden seat on top of a Sussex hill, Bliss and Corinne gazed down on the country home of Max Banda.

They had motored to Lushington early that morning, discovered which was Banda's place by a casual question in the village, and climbed one of the many chalk paths up the three-hundred-foot downland hill to get a perfect bird's-eye view of the house. Corinne, wearing a tweed skirt and a windbreaker and the first pair of walking shoes she'd ever owned, had climbed without complaint, her attention concentrated more on the distant prospect of wealth than the immediate struggle to the summit. Now, alone on the smooth, sheep-grazed hilltop, they could observe the panorama at their feet in undisturbed security. The day, seized on by Bliss the moment he'd heard the morning forecast, was freakishly warm and springlike for early March and ideal for the start of their campaign.

Through a pair of powerful binoculars, Bliss first of all studied the house. It was a modest country residence for a tycoon, but an attractive one—long and white-walled, under new thatch. It stood by itself on a shoulder of hill between two ribbons of minor road that met just above it. The grounds consisted mostly of lawns and shrubbery. One boundary was marked by what appeared to be a small stream, which passed under the more northerly of the two roads by way of a culvert. Bliss could see no sign of the owner, but a woman with gray hair was visible through one of the upper windows, making a bed. Two cars were parked on grass verges close by the house, one on each of the roads. In each car, a man was sitting.

"Guarded fore-and-aft," Bliss said. "They're certainly taking no chances. I expect they open his letters and tap his phone, too."

Presently he switched his attention to the surrounding terrain. The hill on which he and Corinne were sitting was an isolated, flat-topped cone in an otherwise continuous downland ridge. From the fork above the house the road climbed through a gap and wound around the back of the hill in a series of bends before turning off southward in the direction of the sea. It was in one of the bends, out of sight of the house, that the Mercedes was parked. The only other conspicuous features nearby were an unfenced chalk quarry near the fork and a small copse of beech trees a hundred yards or so below the house on the northern road.

Bliss sat pondering for a while. Now that he'd been able to take a good look at the place, he could see both the opportunities and the obstacles much more clearly. The opportunities were better than he'd hoped, but the obstacles were formidable. Before he could take any decisions, he'd need a lot more information.

He raised the binoculars again, concentrating on three things that particularly interested him. First, a ground-floor room at the side of the house, near the

northern road, which had French windows and a piece
of furniture inside that looked like a rolltop desk. Next,
the quarry. It was obviously disused, an abandoned
hole in the hillside, close above the house. Its floor,
Bliss saw, was heavily overgrown with thorn bushes.
Finally, the culvert, and the eastern approaches to it
from the copse.

"Yes," he said, passing the glasses to Corinne. "Not
too unpromising." He felt for a cigarette. "Well, we've
learned as much as we can for the moment. Now all
we can do is wait."

Waiting was no hardship. The day was growing
warmer, the air was deliciously scented, the only
sounds were remote and pleasantly rural. Bliss strolled
about the hilltop, familiarizing himself with the lie of
the land, the pattern of the roads, and the network of
chalk paths. Corinne took off her windbreaker, undid
a button or two, and stretched out on the dry, springy
turf, sunning herself. Presently Bliss joined her on the
grass. "Delectable day!" he said. "Beautiful spot!" He
looked her over, smiling. "Smashing bird . . . !"

Corinne intercepted his straying hand. "Hadn't you
better keep your mind on the job and your eye on the
house?"

"Spoilsport! Maybe you're right, though. Business
before pleasure. . . ." Bliss picked up the glasses again
and resumed his watch.

It was just before noon when the vigil ended. A
movement below brought a sudden exclamation from
Bliss. Corinne sat up. The front door of the house had
opened and a man was coming out.

"There you are," Bliss said. "I win my bet. Max Banda in person. On a lovely spring day; and with damn all else to do he *had* to come out. He's going for a walk, too—look, he's got a stick."

"You're positively clairvoyant." Corinne put on her windbreaker and quickly made up her face. "All right —shall I go?"

"Not yet. Let's see what he does, first."

They watched Banda walk down the drive and out through an open gateway onto the southern road. He paused for a moment by the parked car, as though speaking to the man in it. Then he turned to his right, toward the fork and the gap. After he'd gone about fifty yards, the man got out of the car and strolled slowly after him.

"Just as we thought," Bliss said. "A tail on him all the time. Okay—down to the road and do your stuff. Sure you know your lines?"

Corinne nodded. "Word perfect."

"Fine. Don't forget to give him your best seraglio smile—but keep on walking. Don't let him talk to you. I'll pick you up by the copse in fifteen minutes."

The path down was winding and, in parts, steep. Corinne took it slowly, watching her step, but keeping an eye, too, on the progress of Banda and his shadow. If her timing was good she might be able to get through to the copse without the policeman even see-ing her. If not, she must try to look casual, like someone who'd just got out of a car for a short morning saunter. She knew that the success of the whole plan could de-pend on what happened during the next few minutes, but she wasn't unduly worried. Like Bliss, she knew

her abilities, and this wouldn't be the first time she'd
fixed up a secret assignation with a man.

She skirted the quarry, reached the road and turned
left toward the gap. Now the walkers were out of sight,
hidden by a bend. She adjusted her pace to a leisurely
stroll and came slowly to the bend. She could hear
Banda's stick tapping on the road. A moment later he
rounded the corner. He, too, was strolling. The policeman was well back, still short of the fork.

She took a long breath. She'd got to say a lot of
words in a few vital seconds. Banda was only ten yards
away. Five yards. Almost abreast. He was looking at
her. . . .

She gave him a dazzling smile and said very distinctly as she passed, "Come to the seat on the hill at
three this afternoon, Mr. Banda, and you'll hear something to your advantage." She went on without changing her pace. Banda's stick stopped tapping. She
guessed that he'd stopped and turned. Nothing about
that to arouse suspicion—men often turned to look at
her legs. Anyway, there was no one around to notice.
She quickened her step a little, came to the fork just
before the policeman reached it, and swung off along
the northern road. Good—she'd missed him. The man
in the second police car was writing something in a
book as she passed, and barely glanced up. She strolled
on. She was almost at the copse when Bliss overtook
her in the Mercedes and picked her up.

"Well?" he asked eagerly.

"It worked like a dream," Corinne said. "Timing—
everything. All according to plan."

"Splendid!" Bliss patted the back of her hand as it

lay on the seat. "I can see you and I are going to make a fine team."

"I hope so. The question is, will Banda keep the appointment?"

"He will if he heard you clearly. He'll be too curious not to. Like another bet?"

Corinne smiled. "No, thanks."

Bliss glanced at his watch. "Right—we've just time to go into Lewes and get some lunch."

They were back on the hilltop by half past two. A car with a family in it had preceded them up the road, but Bliss was relieved to see that it hadn't stopped. He and Corinne still had the summit to themselves. Bliss had gambled on that. Anything else would have been bad luck on a weekday in early March.

"Okay," he said, as they reached the seat. "Let's test for sound. You stay here."

Corinne sat down on the seat. Bliss spread his raincoat on the grass about twenty yards away, on the side farthest from the house, and lay down. "How's that?" he asked, raising his voice only a little above normal conversational level.

"I think you should come a bit nearer," Corinne said.

Bliss moved the raincoat five yards closer to the seat and tried again. "Better?"

"Yes, that's about right."

They talked for a few moments, without strain. Then Bliss gave a satisfied nod, and Corinne joined him on the grass.

"Let's hope the guard doesn't decide to sit on the seat with him," she said.

"He's not likely to. He's probably been told to keep his distance."

"What will we do if Banda *doesn't* come?"

Bliss shrugged. "Think of something else. There's always another way."

They began to watch the house. Even through the glasses, there was no sign of any movement. Both the guards appeared to be enjoying an afternoon sleep. The minutes ticked by. Corinne began to grow despondent. "He isn't coming," she said. "I'm sure he isn't." By five minutes to three Bliss was beginning to wonder himself if he'd been too optimistic. "Perhaps he's been held up by something—a telephone call. . . ." Then he suddenly said "Ah!" and pointed. The front door had opened and Banda was coming out. Once more he had his stick with him. Once more, as he set off up the road, one of the plain-clothes men roused himself and fell in behind him. "Who'd be a policeman?" Bliss said.

This time Banda took the first uphill track he came to. He climbed slowly, stopping frequently to look back, as though admiring the view. If his aim was nonchalance, the effect was achieved. The two at the top followed his progress until the shoulder of the hill obscured him. "Right," Bliss said. "Seconds out for round two!" He lay down beside Corinne and clasped her in a loving embrace, but not so loving that he couldn't look past her to see what was happening.

As Banda drew near, Bliss studied him. He was an unusually short man. He had a fine head and a high forehead and looked benevolent and trustworthy, which was no doubt how he'd been able to get away with so much loot. His body was paunchy. "Been hitting the carbohydrates," Bliss murmured. His hair was silver gray and brushed loosely back without a parting. He gave the recumbent couple a long hard look as he approached—particularly Corinne—but he sat down on the seat without speaking.

Bliss fondled Corinne's hair and eyed the distant guard. At the sight of Banda on the seat, the man had stopped, but he was still looking at the lovers. Evidently he decided there was nothing to worry about. After a moment he took a newspaper from his pocket, dropped to the ground, and began to read. He was almost a hundred yards from the seat and well out of earshot. The assignation plan had worked perfectly.

Bliss said, "Can you hear me, Mr. Banda?"

Banda turned his head and nodded.

"Okay. Don't look at us when you talk. My name is Michael Bliss. This is my fiancée, Corinne Lake."

"I think I have met Miss Lake," Banda said. He had a trace of accent, slightly guttural, and a rather stilted way of speaking. "I congratulate you." He sounded as though he meant it.

Bliss snuggled closer to Corinne. "Ignore our antics —they are strictly for the guard. I'll come straight to business. Like you, we live by our wits. Unlike you, we've never been caught. You're going to get anything up to fourteen years. I'm assuming you're sufficiently realistic to know that. Now here's the proposition. For a suitable consideration, I'll undertake to get you out of this country and safely to France—and from there you can go anywhere."

"Impossible!" Banda said.

"Not at all. If you put yourself unreservedly in my hands I can almost guarantee it."

There was a pause. Banda gazed up at a skylark twittering in the blue. In profile, he looked like a rather noble cleric. "I have no passport and my face is known to every policeman and every emigration official in the country. *How* would you get me out?"

"In an oak chest," Bliss said. "It sounds corny, I know, but it'll work. My fiancée and I are planning to live abroad ourselves and the chest will go with us as part of our effects. I'm a prosecution witness in a shooting case and the police are going to help us to clear out quickly after the hearing, for our safety. They're eating out of my hand—they can't do enough for me. That's why it'll work."

Banda swiveled his head sharply to look at Bliss—his first real sign of interest. Then he remembered the guard, and looked away again. "How would you get me away from *here?* I am watched day and night."

"That's something I still have to figure out," Bliss said. "But I've got ideas. Pimpernel's my second name." He smiled down at Corinne and gave her a gentle kiss as the guard glanced across at them.

"Supposing you succeeded," Banda said. "To move on from France, I would have to have a passport."

"I'll get you one."

"A black-market fake, which could land me in trouble at any time? No thank you."

"Not a fake, Mr. Banda—a genuine one. The real McCoy. One you could travel the world with and never lose a moment's sleep."

"That would not be easy to obtain."

"Of course it wouldn't be *easy*. If any of this were easy, the price wouldn't be so high."

"What price are you thinking of?"

"Twenty-five thousand pounds when I produce the passport, to be transferred to a bank in France which I'll name. That'll be a sort of deposit—a payment on account. Once you're safely in France, a further two hundred thousand, to be transferred in the same way."

Banda's profile lost some of its nobility. "Two hundred thousand! You must be out of your mind."

"That's the figure," Bliss said, "and I'm not prepared to haggle. It's a specialist fee for a specialist job. It takes account of the tremendous upheaval we'll have to put up with in our lives, and the considerable risks we'll be running. It's the lowest figure that would make the job worth while. You could call it the market price."

"What makes you think I have that sort of money?"

"According to the police evidence," Bliss said, "you pinched nearly two million pounds from your trusting shareholders and if you haven't managed to conjure a good slice of it away somewhere you're not the financial wizard I think you are."

Banda grunted.

"Just one word of warning, though. Don't imagine you can fool us. Once we're in France, we'll stick by you till the full amount is paid. If you try to welsh on us—well, I'm not given to violence as a rule, but in those circumstances I'd probably lose my temper and beat the living daylights out of you. So watch it! You know how you're fixed financially. If for any reason, technical or otherwise, you can't or won't pay, now's the time to say so, and we'll forget the whole thing."

"It's a ridiculous figure, my friend."

"For liberty? For fourteen years of life and love instead of fourteen years in the nick? What's money to you? What good is it going to be to you? When you come out, you'll be a broken old man. Still, if that's your view . . ." Bliss raised himself on an elbow and looked down at Corinne. "I guess we should be going, dear—the grass is getting damp."

"Wait!" Banda said. "You are too hasty. Of course, you are right—the figure, however preposterous, is a secondary matter. But I do not believe you can do what you say. The obstacles appear to me insuperable. I would need to know a great deal more before I could take your proposition seriously."

"In time, you'll know everything," Bliss said, "but this isn't the moment for details. All I'm seeking now is your reaction to the principle of the thing. What have you got to lose by playing along with us?"

"At this stage, nothing."

"At every stage, nothing. Or almost nothing. A couple of sureties and a small deposit—that's your maximum stake. Peanuts! If the plan turns out a flop you won't have to pay the main sum, and even if you're caught you'll be no worse off. You're going to be jailed anyway. They won't add thumbscrews for attempted escape."

"That is true."

"All right, then. So—are you interested?"

"I am *interested*—naturally."

"Are you interested enough to go ahead and see what happens next?"

"Perhaps . . ."

Bliss gave an exaggerated sigh of relief. "In that case," he said, "there's a whole string of questions I must ask you."

"Very well. Ask them."

"Do you plan to stay down here till your trial?"

"That is my intention."

"What's your domestic setup? Was that a housekeeper I saw at a window?"

"No. My housekeeper left me. A woman comes in daily from the village. Not a very efficient woman, but the best I could get. She cooks my lunch, and leaves a cold supper for me."

"A Spartan life, eh? Still, it's probably better than Wormwood Scrubs! So she's never around in the evenings?"

"No."

"Is anyone around in the evenings? Lawyers, accountants, visitors, friends . . . ?"

"The lawyers come in the daytime. Also the accountants. A man in my position has no friends. I am alone."

"Wait till I dry my tears! Okay—now about the police guards. Do they ever go inside the house?"

"Never."

"Do they patrol?"

"Not in any regular way. They walk up and down the roads from time to time. They have no beat, if that is what you mean."

"When do they change guard?"

"At ten o'clock, six o'clock and two o'clock."

"H'm—you rate quite a squad, don't you! Do the same men turn up at the same times?"

"Usually, yes."

"Do you ever talk to any of them?"

"Occasionally."

"You're on friendly terms with them?"

"Courteous and correct, I would say. I give them no trouble and they try not to bother me unduly."

"Fine. Now about your own way of life. Which room do you mostly occupy in the evenings?"

"Usually my study. That is on the ground floor at the side."

"The one with the French doors opening on the lawn?"

"Yes."

"Do the curtains completely cover the windows?"

"Yes."

"Do you usually draw them after dark, when you're there?"

"Yes."

"What time do you dine?"

"If you can call it dining—about seven-fifteen."

"Do you sit up late at night?"

"Often until one o'clock. I am a poor sleeper."

"You surprise me! Do you read in bed?"

"Quite often. Sometimes almost till daybreak."

"Good. Have you a portable radio?"

"Yes."

"Do you play it much?"

"From time to time, when there is good music."

"I see you've got television, too. Where do you keep the set?"

"I have two sets. One is in the study, and the other in my bedroom."

Bliss gave a satisfied nod. "Now, that stream that runs through your grounds, is there much water in it?"

"At the moment, almost none. This has been a dry season."

"I noticed it runs under the road through a culvert. Could a man get through that culvert?"

"I would think so—it is very large. When the stream is in spate, it needs to be."

"Well, let's hope the weather holds. What's your height?"

"Five feet four inches."

"And your weight?"

"One hundred and seventy-six pounds."

"Are you in good health? No sudden attacks of anything—asthma, heart trouble, epilepsy?"

"I am in excellent health, thank you, all things considered."

"If you grew a mustache, what would it be like?"

"It would be gray, and rather bristly."

"What's your telephone number?"

"Lushington 438. But I think . . ."

"*I* know—someone listens. Right. Now if you're still interested, some general instructions. . . . Don't do exactly the same things every day. Use your study some evenings, but not all. Read till the early hours some nights, but not every night. Have the telly on in your bedroom sometimes. Stroll in the garden after dinner sometimes. Talk to the police occasionally. Do a little of everything. Keep them foxed. The main thing is not to create a fixed pattern, because I'm not sure yet what pattern we'll need."

"I understand," Banda said.

"Oh, yes—and from now on pretend you're going a little deaf. Don't overdo it, but ask the police to repeat things occasionally. And play your radio a little louder each time. Turn up the TV sound a bit. Okay?"

"What is the point of that?"

"I'll tell you some other time. Now for our first move. I'll need to take a photograph of you for your new

passport and get your signature on some forms. That
means I'll have to come secretly to the house. After
dark, of course."

"With the guards watching? I am sure they are particularly alert at night."

"I don't doubt it, but we can get over that. Here's
the plan. On the day I'm coming, I shall dial your
telephone number from a local call box at precisely
seven p.m. It won't be for some time—but make sure
you're at hand to take a call at that time each day.
When you lift the receiver, say 'Lushington 438.' I
shall then ring off without speaking. That will be the
signal. Before you dine you will make sure that the
lights are off in your study and that one of the French
doors is left slightly ajar. At five minutes to eight you
will go out by the front door, stroll around to the back,
and engage the guard there in conversation. As long
as he's got you safely under his eye he won't be worrying about anything else. At eight o'clock I shall slip
into the study through the open door, shut it behind
me, and draw the curtains. At five past eight you will
return to the house by the front door and join me in
the study. Naturally, I shall choose an evening when
the weather is good. Now is that all clear?"

"It is." Banda gazed out into space. "I am bound to
say I have little hope—but I shall do as you say. You
are, I must admit, a remarkable man."

"I'm unique," Bliss said. "Pity you didn't have me on
your board of directors! Now you'd better go, or that
cop will be getting suspicious."

"When shall I hear the rest of your plan?"

"Later—much later. For the moment, just leave

everything to me. Where ignorance is Bliss, you know!
Okay—see you on the ice!"

Banda got to his feet, cast a slightly nostalgic glance
at Corinne sprawled on the ground, and set off back
toward the guard.

Corinne stirred. "Do you mind, Mike—I'm absolutely
flattened."

Bliss grinned down at her. "After all your experience," he said, "I'm surprised you even notice!"

They stayed on the hilltop just long enough to let
Banda and the guard disappear from view. Then they
descended by a southern path that brought them
quickly to the Mercedes.

"Well," Corinne said, as she began to repair some of
the damage Bliss had done to her makeup, "We seem
to have been given the go-ahead, don't we?"

Bliss nodded. "Very satisfactory. Now we can really
get cracking."

"What did you think of him?"

"I thought he seemed very docile. Not surprising, of
course—there's nothing like misfortune to induce a little humility. If he goes on doing as he's told, we
shouldn't have much trouble."

"I mean, what did you think of him as a man?"

"As a *man* . . . ! You must be joking."

"No—really."

"Well—I thought he was revolting."

"Did you? I thought he was rather impressive. Quiet
and dignified. Sort of monumental. And he has a most
distinguished face."

"Yes—with a row of chins under it. And pudgy hands.

He's a gross type. Imagine him gadding about with young girls at his time of life!"

"Lots of men do."

"They're welcome. Personally I'd hate it. Feeling you'd got to be on your toes all the time, when you were so fat you couldn't even catch sight of them. Lascivious old so-and-so! You should have seen the way he looked at you."

Corinne smiled. "It couldn't be that you're jealous?"

"Me, jealous?" Bliss said. "That's a laugh!"

Corinne lay on Bliss's sofa, relaxing with a cigarette and a drink after one of the most physically arduous days she could remember. The time was nine o'clock. Bliss, still full of energy and eager to press on with the job, was already tackling the problem of getting a passport for Banda. He had brought out an ancient but still serviceable typewriter from the glory hole and was busy drafting an advertisement.

He tapped away for some minutes without speaking. Then he sat back. "How does this sound to you?" he asked. "'Gentleman, fifty, contemplating round-world trip, seeks male companion of similar age. Generous salary and all expenses paid. British subjects only. Previous travel experience not essential.'"

Corinne reflected. "Why 'British subjects only'?"

"We'll need the chap's birth certificate to send up with the form, and that'll give us an excuse to ask for it."

"Ah, yes, of course. Very clever."

"And the bit about 'travel experience not essential' is because we want someone who's never held a passport before. That should sift them out."

Corinne nodded, and was silent for a moment. "I'm

just wondering if you haven't made the offer sound too attractive," she said. "You don't want a great stack of replies on your hall table all on the same day. Someone might get curious."

"That's a thought. Okay, I'll slim it down a bit."

"I'm not sure about 'gentleman seeks male companion of similar age,' either. You'll probably get a lot of answers from bright, aging queers. I thought you wanted someone ordinary and a bit dim."

"Quite true. Right, I'll have another bash." Bliss did some more tapping. "There—how do you like this version? 'Widower, fifty, obliged travel abroad for health reasons, seeks companion/help (male) of similar age. Salary small but all expenses paid. British subjects only. State nursing/travel experience, if any. Box number so-and-so.'"

"That's much better," Corinne said. "Now you should get some earnest little man who needs a roof over his head and won't be inclined to ask too many questions. Yes, I approve of that."

"Good. Now, what paper shall we put it in? Not the *Times*, obviously. Perhaps not the *Telegraph*, either— bit too classy. How about the *Evening News?*"

"Yes, I should think so. Under 'Situations Vacant.'"

Bliss made a fair copy of the advertisement and typed out a covering letter to the newspaper. He gave the address as 15 Bampton Gardens, N.W.3, without a flat number. He signed the letter, after a moment's thought, "George Lennox," using his left hand—a method of disguising his writing that he'd long ago perfected. He addressed the envelope, sealed it, stamped it, and touched it with his lips. "Good luck, mate!"

"You could post it in one of those late-collection

boxes when you take me home," Corinne said. "Then they'll get it first thing in the morning."

"Good idea. By the way, would you mind dropping in at the passport office some time and getting a set of forms for a first-passport application? It's only a matter of picking them up off a table, but I don't particularly want to be seen around there myself at the moment."

"Yes, all right," Corinne said. "I'll look in tomorrow."

"And while you're about it, you might buy a thirty-shilling postal order. We'll need that later."

"Certainly, sir. Always happy to be useful."

"Useful!" Bliss said. "You're going to be worth your weight in gold to me."

Corinne smiled. "I certainly hope so. After all, that's just about what I'm going to cost you!"

In the morning Bliss decided to write an article. The subject was one that wouldn't normally have occurred to him, and his material was so thin that he doubted whether any newspaper would be interested. But that didn't matter. The important thing was that the attempt should have been made, the article sent off. Then he would have a complete answer to what might otherwise be an embarrassing question. Bliss always aimed to be one jump ahead of the opposition; to foresee criticism, and forestall it.

He had barely put the first sheet in the typewriter when Inspector Kirby rang up and asked if he might look in again. He would like, he said, to discuss a few points relating to Bliss's evidence and to give him the latest news on the progress of the committal arrangements. Bliss had the feeling that these were matters which could easily have been discussed on the phone,

and that what Kirby really wanted was to check on his
witness's morale and make sure there was no backslid-
ing. However, the visit suited him very well. It would
give him an opportunity to put in some useful background work.

Kirby arrived at half-past eleven. He seemed in very
good spirits and was noticeably less official in his manner than on previous occasions. Bliss responded in the
same informal way. After all, they were both on the
same side now. Practically colleagues!

"Have a chair, Inspector. I was just thinking of taking a glass of white wine—how about joining me before we get down to business? It's a rather special
vintage."

"That's very kind of you," Kirby said.

"I won't be a moment." Bliss went into the kitchen
and returned with a frosted bottle, two gleaming
glasses, a white napkin and a patent corkscrew, on a
tray. "I always think a little wine goes down well at
this time of day." He grinned. "Or at any other time,
come to that!" He opened the bottle carefully, wiped
the inside of the neck with the napkin, filled the two
glasses, held one of them up to the light, and passed it
to Kirby. "Try that, Inspector."

Kirby sipped the wine. "H'm—very nice. Most refreshing."

"I thought you'd like it. It's a Medderheimer Edel-
burg Riesling, 1961 vintage. Are you up in wine at all?"

"I can't say I am, sir—but I'm quite ready to learn.
Always glad to store up a bit of new information."

"Ah, yes—packing away the other man's expertise
for future use, eh? Well, I think you'll be interested in
this wine. It's called ice wine and it's quite a rarity. As

a matter of fact, you only get it a few times in a century. It happens when there's a very late harvesting of the grapes—so late that they're actually frozen on the vine and are still frozen when they're pressed. The essentials of the grape are concentrated and a very outstanding wine results."

"Most interesting," Kirby said. He took another sip. "I can see you're a connoisseur, Mr. Bliss."

"I try to be. Wine's been a hobby of mine for years."

"Do you keep a cellar?"

"A small one. Not literally, of course. That's one of the drawbacks about living in a flat. Wine should be kept at an even temperature of not more than fifty-five degrees, otherwise it matures too fast, so one does really need an underground cellar. When Corinne and I settle in Provence, I'll see we get one. Fortunately I've got a large cool cupboard here, which is the next best thing. Well, now—to work, eh?"

"Yes," Kirby said. "To begin with, it looks as though the committal proceedings will be a little later than we expected. The prosecution isn't quite ready, so there'll be at least one more adjournment. This is the position. . . ."

Bliss leaned forward, concentrated and attentive, his role now that of the earnest listener. Privately he was congratulating himself on his skillful introduction of the wine theme. And thinking that a little delay in the Olsen case was just what he needed. *He* wasn't quite ready, either.

During the next day or two Bliss kept a watchful eye on the post. Until he got a suitable reply to his advertisement there was little more he could do to further his plan. He had some useful discussions with Corinne about various problems that would arise in the later stages, and one or two recreational sessions with her at the flat, though he was really too preoccupied at the moment for bedroom athletics. He was very much aware that in a few weeks' time the evenings would be getting dangerously light and that the timetable of action, when it was finally drawn up, would be tight.

It was on the morning of the fourth day that the first replies arrived at Bampton Gardens. They had been forwarded in one large envelope, addressed in neat typescript to "George Lennox Esq." Bliss, having watched the postman enter the building, was able to whisk it off the hall table before anyone else in the house had a chance to see it.

There were eight letters in the envelope, all from the London area or the home counties. Bliss discarded five of them straight away, since they mentioned previous travel abroad. He rejected two more, after some thought, because the writers sounded too alert and knowledgeable to be a safe bet. The one he finally settled down to answer was very much what he'd been hoping for. It was from an address in South Croydon, and it ran:

Dear Sir,
    In reply to your advertisement in the *Evening News* I beg to apply for the post you offer. I am a male nurse forty-nine years old. I have had hospital experience as an orderly and done nursing training and I have been working with private patients since 1960. I can supply any references you wish. I am a cheerful reliable person easy to get on with and with no bad habits. I am a British subject born in Rugby. I have never been to a foreign country but

am sure I would enjoy the experience. Please state what the salary will be and when you intend to start your trip and how long it will last. Also I would like to hear about your state of health, so I will know what is required. I will be free to come to you from the end of May.

Yours truly,
Harold Lever

Bliss typed a reply at once, using his ancient machine.

Dear Mr. Lever,

Thank you very much for your letter of March 12th in reply to my advertisement. I like the sound of your application and I feel you may be just the man I am looking for. I suffer from asthma and a little heart trouble, but nothing, I think, to worry about. All I need is a companion who will relieve me of some of the strain of day-to-day living. The appointment will carry a salary of £1,000 per annum, plus expenses, and in the first place will be for twelve months—though if we get on well together it could be for much longer. I would be obliged if you would submit a copy of your birth certificate—not that I doubt what you say for a moment, but on a previous occasion I was misled about the nationality of a gentleman I employed, who turned out to be a Hungarian! I will then write to you again with regard to a meeting and taking up your references, and of course I will let you have references too if you want them. Meanwhile it may interest you to know that I hope to spend a good part of the twelve months in the south of France, which has a very good climate and which I am sure you will like. I myself shall not be ready to leave until early summer, so if you are free around the end of May that will be just right.

Yours sincerely,
George Lennox

The reply came by return post.

Dear Mr. Lennox,

I was very pleased to hear that you approved of my application and I enclose my birth certificate which shows I am a genuine British subject. I am sure I will enjoy the trip you mention as well as being a great help to you and I look forward to hearing further from you.

Yours truly,
Harold Lever

P.S. The salary is satisfactory.

Bliss studied the birth certificate. It was, he saw, the original document, now much worn and yellowing at the edges. He read through the particulars. Christian names—Arthur Harold. Born December 28, 1919. Place of birth, 11a Birdhurst Road, Rugby. Name of father, James Thomas Lever. Name of mother, Kathleen Mary Lever, formerly Green. Father's profession, plumber. Birth registered January 15, 1920.

Bliss sat thinking. The sooner he could get the certificate back to Lever, the less chance there'd be of any suspicion arising about its use. And there was no telling how long the passport office would keep it, if he sent it off with the application. Also, Bliss didn't know if it was their practice to put some mark or stamp on birth certificates submitted to them. It should be, of course— it was a security precaution that Bliss himself would have thought of. But authority was always dim. Still, on the whole, perhaps it would be better not to risk it.

He got out his old typewriter again and typed a letter to the registrar at Rugby. It purported to be from Harold Lever, whose present address was 15 Bampton Gardens, N.W.3. It gave Harold Lever's place and

date of birth and parents' names, and requested that a
copy of his birth certificate be sent to him as soon as
possible. Bliss looked up the fee in an almanac, went
out and bought a postal order, and dispatched the letter. The operation would take a little longer this way
than if he'd gone straight to Somerset House with the
particulars, but it was safer than a public appearance.

Back at the flat, he tore all the advertisement appli-
cations into small pieces and flushed them away in the
bathroom.

The copy of the birth certificate arrived just thirty-
six hours later. Bliss collected it from the hall table
with some other items of mail, checked it over in the
study, and went gleefully to his desk to compose a final
letter:

Dear Mr. Lever,
    I am writing to you on behalf of Mr. George Len-
nox, with whom you have recently been in correspondence about a post as help/companion. I am
very sorry to have to tell you that Mr. Lennox yesterday suffered a severe heart attack and is now in
hospital. You will appreciate that all his plans have
had to be canceled and it is now most unlikely that
he will be able to go abroad. I am sure he would
wish me to convey his regret for any disappointment
you may have been caused. I am returning the birth
certificate which you were kind enough to submit.

                            Yours sincerely,
                            A. E. Stanton
                            Secretary to Mr. Lennox

With the duplicate birth certificate safely in hand,
Bliss began at once to prepare for the next operation.
First, a check on the weather. A call to the Meteoro-

logical Office for a special forecast brought the information that no rain was expected to fall in Sussex for at
least twenty-four hours. The evening would be cloudy
and mild. The sort of weather, Bliss felt, that would
allow Banda to take a stroll on his lawn after dinner
without causing the slightest comment. So tonight was
the night! Bliss rang Corinne, told her he had news
which he couldn't discuss on the phone, and asked her
to call around in the early afternoon.

During the morning he drove into the West End
and visited a theatrical costumer's near Charing Cross.
He wanted, he said, a bristly gray mustache. "High
jinks at the church hall tonight," he told the girl assistant, with a grin. He chose one that wasn't too mili-
tary, remembering Banda's contours, and allowed the
girl to fix it experimentally to his upper lip with a little
gum arabic. It was, he decided, just the thing. He also
bought a pair of horn-rimmed spectacles with plain
glass instead of lenses—a pair which the assistant
thought were slightly on the loose side for him, but
which he nevertheless took. They would fit Banda's
face perfectly. He lunched frugally at a pub counter
and returned to the flat with his purchases.

In the afternoon he changed into an old clerical gray
suit that would make him almost invisible in the dark.
He also changed his town shoes for a pair of crepe-
soled brogues which would soften his footsteps. Afterward he packed a small attaché case. He put in a
camera, flash bulbs and lamp; a spare film; a hairbrush
and comb; a bottle of hair oil; the mustache and gum
arabic and spectacles; and, in a large envelope to
keep them clean, the passport application forms that
Corinne had obtained for him.

So far, so good. He looked around. Now what was that other little job he'd made a mental note of? Ah, yes—the bottle. Better do that while he remembered. He went to the cabinet behind the bar, took out a bottle of wine, carried it to the bathroom, and weighed it on the scales. Just under three pounds. Now he wouldn't be caught out when the time came.

He stood for a while in front of the bathroom mirror, trying out a few facial contortions. Drawing in his cheeks to make them look hollow, stretching out his upper lip, compressing his mouth. Obviously the thing mustn't be overdone. He was still experimenting when Corinne let herself into the flat with the key he had given her.

She gazed at him in astonishment through the open bathroom door. "Mike! Are you all right?"

"Perfectly," he called. "Just practicing."

"Heavens, I thought you were having a fit!" She hung up her coat and joined him. "Well, what's the position?"

"Oh, very upstanding. The birth certificate came this morning. The correspondence with Mr. H. Lever is now closed."

"Really? That's wonderful. Congratulations!" Corinne was beginning to feel the sort of respect for Bliss that a commander might enjoy among troops he invariably led to victory. Every new ploy seemed to come off. "So now you're ready to see Banda again?"

"Yes, I'm going down this afternoon. I won't feel happy till I've got that photograph. Actually I was wondering whether to use a bit of makeup on him? Paint him up a little before he poses?"

"I wouldn't advise it," Corinne said. "You'll probably daub him in all the wrong places and he'll finish up looking like a Pierrot. If there's any making up to be done, I suggest I do it in France."

"M'm—perhaps you're right. Anyway, I've got the mustache and glasses—they should be enough."

"How do you feel about going to the house? Aren't you scared?"

Bliss looked at her in surprise. "Scared? Why should I be scared? I'm looking forward to it."

"Suppose someone sees you?"

"I'll take jolly good care they don't."

"Well, I'll keep my fingers crossed! Will you give me a ring when . . ." Corinne broke off as her glance fell on the weighing machine. "What on earth are you doing with a bottle of wine in the bathroom?"

"Just working out what I'll tell old Hawkeye. There's so much to think of, I really will have to make a list."

"Are you sure you can cope? It's going to be pretty tricky, isn't it, managing Banda and Kirby both at the same time?"

Bliss grinned. "'If you can't ride two horses at once you shouldn't be in the bloody circus!' Don't worry— everything's under control."

It was a few minutes short of seven when Bliss pulled up outside an empty phone box in Lushington village. He switched on the car radio and waited for the seven o'clock time signal. As the pips went he slipped into the box and dialed Banda's number.

Almost at once, Banda came on the line. "Lushington 438," he said, a trifle breathlessly. His trace of accent was more noticeable on the phone. Bliss rang off without speaking and quickly left the box.

Outside, he paused, looking up at the sky. The forecast had been an accurate one. The rain had kept off but there was a good deal of cloud, which suited him well. Dusk would be early. He got back into the car and briefly studied his inch-to-the-mile map, refreshing his memory about approaches to Banda's house from the village. Then he drove slowly to the copse and parked the Mercedes in among the trees. A car went by, already showing its sidelights. He wouldn't have long to wait now. He was keyed up and eager to get moving. In spite of what he'd said to Corinne he had the feeling that the next hour was going to be distinctly dodgy, and he couldn't afford any mistake. If he *was* discovered, with that bag of tricks he'd brought with him, it would take more than fast talk to get him out of trouble. It would be the end. So he'd better be careful.

At seven-forty he took the attaché case from the back seat of the Mercedes and made his way through the trees to the edge of the road. No car light was visible in either direction. He walked quickly to a field gate he'd already marked down for use, climbed it, dropped to the grassy meadow on the other side, and put the hedge between himself and the road. Now he felt safe from observation. He set off up the sloping field, keeping as close to the hedge as he could. The ground was hard but the going was rough, with treacherous holes where cattle had trodden in wet weather, and he had to pick his steps with care. He negotiated another gate into a higher field, the one opposite the house, and felt his way cautiously forward toward the stream.

Darkness had fallen by the time he reached it. He

glanced at the luminous dial of his watch. Ten minutes to eight. Ahead, through the thin screen of the hedge, he could see a faint glow by the roadside. The interior light of one of the guard cars. He could also hear some movement on the road. Slow footsteps. The measured tread of the law. He began to lower himself, inch by careful inch, into the bed of the stream. The ground was squelchy at the bottom, but there was only a trickle of running water. Clutching the attaché case in his left hand, he groped with his right for the culvert. In a moment he touched brick. He traced the outline of the opening with his fingers. The roof of the culvert was about four feet from the bed. He bent low and crept through it without difficulty. He was now at the extreme edge of Banda's garden, with no fence or obstacle between him and the house. He paused at the mouth of the culvert, listening.

In a moment he heard a door open. The front door, by the sound of it. More footsteps, this time on gravel. Coming nearer. Then away again. Over toward a rustic gate that opened onto the road. Bliss remembered seeing the gate from the hilltop. A latch clicked. A voice spoke. Banda's. Loud and clear in the evening hush. "Do you think we are going to have rain, officer?" Dangerously close, but the best that could be hoped for. A steady flow of conversation, now. And just eight o'clock. Bully for Banda! Bliss emerged from the culvert, hand outstretched to the right. A grassy bank, rising from the stream. Flowers growing in it. Daffodils. Better avoid those. Bits of rock, too, that could easily be dislodged. With infinite care Bliss felt his way up the slope, using the attaché case to steady himself. When the ground leveled out he paused again.

The layout of the garden was clear in his mind. Ahead of him was the sweep of lawn he'd seen through the glasses. The study was just round the corner of the house, to the left. Well, this was it! He tiptoed swiftly across the grass, turned the corner, saw the dark glass of the study doors, and crept up to them. The right-hand door was ajar. He eased it gently outward and slipped inside. With scarcely a sound he closed the door behind him and fastened it. He drew the curtains, making sure there was no chink for light to get through. Then he put his case down, and waited.

Very soon he heard more sounds. The slam of the front door. Footsteps in the hall. Footsteps in the passage. Then a sharp line of light cut the darkness as the study door opened a fraction. "Okay," Bliss said softly, "you can switch on. The curtains are drawn." A plump white hand reached in and clicked the light on. Banda closed the door behind him and gazed, rather incredulously, at his visitor.

"So!" he said. "You came."

"Keep your voice down! Of course I came. Did you think I wouldn't?"

"I had almost given you up when you telephoned."

"You should have more faith. I told you it would be quite a while before I got in touch with you again. I've had a lot of very important correspondence to attend to."

"I see. . . . And how are things going?"

"Like a bomb."

Banda's mouth turned down. "I can think of happier similes."

"Don't worry," Bliss said. "It's the opposition that's going to be shaken."

"I am still very skeptical, my friend."

"Be as skeptical as you like," Bliss said, "as long as you don't let it hold things up. We've a great deal to do. First, the photograph." He opened the attaché case and took out the bottle of hair oil. "Here—soak your hair well with this. And try not to spill any. We don't want to leave traces on the carpet."

Banda hesitated, then shrugged. "I will try to believe you know what you are doing." He poured oil liberally over his head and rubbed it in. The oil made his gray hair appreciably darker.

"That's fine," Bliss said. He produced the brush and comb from his case. "Now let's see what we can do about changing the style." He combed out the oily strands, made a parting at the crown, brushed the sides hard back, and slicked them down as close to the head as he could get them. "Yes, that makes a difference. Now try this mustache. Not too much gum."

"A charade!" Banda muttered. "That is what it is—a charade. I cannot take it seriously." All the same, he fixed the mustache to his upper lip. Bliss adjusted it and touched it lightly with oil so that it matched the hair. "You'll be able to grow a proper one when you get to France," he said.

"Okay—now the glasses." Banda put them on. The frames fitted him perfectly.

Bliss stood back again. "Well, that's certainly a transformation—I doubt if your own shareholders would recognize you! Now let's get the pose right. Look straight at me. Tilt your head down slightly—I want to cut out a few of those chins. Not too much. Now press your lips together. That's splendid. Horrible, but different. Hold it like that, will you?"

Bliss opened up his camera, put a new bulb in the flash lamp, and studied Banda through the view finder. "Head up just a bit. Right." He pressed the trigger. Banda blinked as the flash bulb went off. "Try and keep your eyes open," Bliss said. "We'll have a couple more." Twice more the light flashed. "That's better. And one for luck. Good. One of those should be okay." Briskly, Bliss packed the camera away.

Banda glanced nervously at the window. "I hope no one saw the flashes." Sweat glistened on his forehead.

"No one could see through those curtains," Bliss said. "Anyway, what do you have to be jittery about? If the cops came right in, you could laugh in their faces— which is more than I could. Something wrong with your nerve?"

"I am not used to these cloak-and-dagger activities."

"You'll get used to them," Bliss said.

"I very much doubt it. Is that all we have to do?"

"Not by a long chalk. You're about to take on a new identity." Bliss produced the passport forms. "I left them for you to fill out as you've got to sign them—it looks better if everything's in one hand. Got a pen? I'll tell you what to put."

Banda glanced through the forms. "Do you wish me to disguise my writing?"

"It might be safer. Won't be the first time, will it! But remember the signature you use will be yours for ever after. Right, let's get started."

Banda sat down at his desk. Bliss leaned over his shoulder. "Particulars of applicant, first. Like it or not, your name in future is going to be Lever. L-E-V-E-R— that's right. Christian names in full—Arthur Harold. I guess I'll call you 'Art' for short! Place and country of birth—Rugby, England. Date of birth—December 28, 1919. Single, married, widowed or divorced—well, you can please yourself what you say about that. Address —15 Bampton Gardens, N.W.3. Occupation?—I'd suggest something like 'shopkeeper.' It'll explain why you haven't been abroad before—always stuck behind the counter. Or perhaps you'd prefer something more specific? How about 'haberdasher'? With that mustache you somehow look like a haberdasher." Banda shrugged again, and filled in the space.

They went on through the items, Bliss still instructing. "Countries to be visited—well, you might as well tell the truth and say France—it's the obvious place for a first trip. Purpose of journey—flight from justice. . . ."

Banda looked up. "You have an extraordinary sense of humor, Mr. Bliss."

"I'm afraid so," Bliss said. "It all comes of being a Baptist in my youth. Okay, say 'pleasure.' Now date of departure—I'd make it March 30th, that'll hurry them up. Fine. And this little mauve form. I shouldn't worry about special peculiarities, no one ever does. Signature at the bottom—and on the other form, too. Harold Lever, don't forget." Bliss took the forms and checked them over as Banda laid down his pen. "Yes, they seem in order. A most convincing application, I'd say."

"What about the countersignatures?" Banda asked.

"They'll be taken care of."

"And the birth certificate?"

"I've already got it. You don't have to worry about a thing. Oh—I'd like one more signature." Bliss produced a plain sheet of typing paper. "At the bottom, here.

That's for the covering letter, in case I send one. Good." He put the forms back in the big envelope and closed his case. "Well, I guess that's all for now. You may as well hang on to the mustache and glasses, but don't forget to bring them with you on D-day. When the passport's ready I'll phone you again and we'll go through the same routine we used tonight. But better make it at 7:15 for the phone call and 8:15 for getting into the house—the evenings will be lighter."

"When is this likely to be?" Banda asked. "Assuming that it happens."

"Maybe in a couple of weeks—maybe longer. It all depends on the passport office—I'll be in their hands. But don't agitate yourself—I shall come. Now you'd better go and get that oil off your hair before anyone sees you." Bliss gave a final glance around the room. "The carpet ought to have a bit of a brush, too—I seem to have brought some chalk in. We don't want your cleaning woman to start getting ideas." He picked up his case. "Right—I'm off, then."

"Do you wish me to talk to the guard again?"

"Not twice in an evening, we mustn't overdo it. Take your radio upstairs, turn on some loud music, and open a window. That'll keep the cops happy, and the noise will cover me. I'll manage—I know the layout now. See you in Philippi, Mr. Lever!"

Banda gave a slow headshake, as though the whole affair was more than he could cope with. "You are, indeed, unique!" he said. He switched off the study light and went out, closing the door behind him. Bliss waited in the darkness. In a moment or two the sound of orchestral music reached him from the upper floor. He parted the curtains to the sound of trumpets and opened one of the French doors to the crash of cymbals. He could just make out the interior lights of the guard car beyond the garden hedge. A slight movement in the car showed that the guard was there. Probably wishing it was ten o'clock . . . Bliss slipped through the door, pushed it almost shut behind him, crossed the lawn in a few quick strides, and lowered himself to the stream. In seconds he was through the culvert and on his way down the field to the parked Mercedes.

It had been a piece of cake!

He could hardly wait now to see how the photographs had turned out. Back at the flat he delayed only long enough to telephone Corinne and tell her he was safely back, as she'd asked him to do. Then he got down to work in the glory hole—a place he'd used for developing films on several previous occasions when he'd photographed something that wasn't entirely suitable for the eyes of others. With a small folding table set up to hold his trays of chemicals, a red bulb in the lamp socket, and a plugged-in fan to stir up the warm air, the cupboard served very well as an improvised darkroom.

He emerged after half an hour, sweating but triumphant. The negatives looked good. He dried them quickly in front of a blower, ran off a print of each, and sat down to study them.

The first picture, the one with the eyes half shut, was useless even by the unexacting standards of the passport office, and could be discarded. The second and third were passable. The fourth, the "one for luck," was excellent, and Bliss made the necessary two copies of it. He was particularly pleased with the effect he'd achieved in it by foreshortening the forehead and the chins. The angle had been just right. The face in the picture, though recognizably Banda's to anyone who'd closely observed him, was yet sufficiently different from his published photographs to get him past any continental frontier post without a second glance. If, when Banda reached France, he adjusted his appearance to fit the picture, growing his bristly mustache, disciplining his loose locks and using his glasses when crossing frontiers, he should have no trouble at all.

Once more, Bliss could pride himself on having done a first-class job.

He checked that the prints he'd made were within the regulation passport size limits, destroyed all the photographic debris except his chosen negative, which he'd keep as a precaution until the passport came through, pegged up the prints to dry, cleared up in the cupboard, and turned in for a well-earned night's sleep.

Corinne was around in her Mini at eleven o'clock next morning, eager to hear about the night's adventure. With a complacent grin, Bliss produced the photographs. "There's the old boy's phiz—for better or worse."

Corinne studied the print. "It's marvelous," she said, after a moment. "Hardly flattering, of course, but it's very clever. I do congratulate you. How did the trip go?"

"Like clockwork, as far as I was concerned." Bliss gave her a racy account of his evening out. "Banda wasn't too happy. He's short on guts, and anyway he still doesn't believe I can pull this thing off. He does what he's told in a sort of daze. I don't think he quite knows what's hit him."

"At least he's cooperating," Corinne said. "That's the main thing. So what's the next step?"

"Getting the forms off." Bliss opened his case and took out the envelope. "Banda's handwriting, my dictation. Best bit of fiction I've read in years. Like to look?"

Corinne took the forms and glanced through them. "M'm—most impressive."

"So all we need now is the countersignatures."

"Aren't they supposed to be by a doctor or lawyer or someone like that?"

"Yes, someone of standing. In this case it'll be a bank officer—complete with rubber stamp."

"How will you get that?"

"I've already got it. I'm a 'picker-up of unconsidered trifles,' I'm afraid. Come and look." Bliss went to his desk, took out a large black deed box, and unlocked it. It contained, *inter alia*, a variety of business letter headings and hotel notepapers, an assortment of labeled keys, and at least a dozen different rubber stamps. "I must remember to get rid of this lot before we clear out," he said. "With luck, I shan't need them again." He rummaged among the stamps. "Here we are —from my local bank."

"When did you take it?"

"Oh, a couple of years ago. You know the Bliss family motto—'Be prepared.'"

"Didn't they miss it?"

"If they did, they still went on using similar stamps." Bliss gave a reminiscent grin. "It was damn funny, actually. There'd been one or two holdups in the district and the whole bank staff were providing an escort for some bags of money that were being put in a van. One of them had a truncheon—looked pretty self-conscious, I remember. Anyway, they were so busy guarding the money that no one noticed me slip my hand under a grille and remove the stamp. Rather a pleasing incident, I thought. Right, now let's complete these forms."

With Corinne looking on, Bliss filled in the counter-signature space on the main form, writing with his left hand and certifying that Harold Lever had been known to him personally for five years. He signed "F. E. Childs," wrote "Bank Officer" beside the signature, filled in an address and the date, inked the stamp on a pad, and pressed it firmly in the appropriate spot.

"Did you make the name up?" Corinne asked.

Bliss looked shocked. "Nothing so slovenly. Childs works in my bank. He witnessed my signature on some documents a few months ago—that's how I know his private address. Now for the photograph. Let's see —what's the phrasing?" He consulted the "Notes for Guidance" that Corinne had brought from the passport office with the forms, then wrote on the back of one of the prints, "I certify that this is a true likeness of the applicant, Mr. Harold Lever," and signed "F. E. Childs."

He sat back. "That does it, then. Did you get the thirty-bob postal order?"

"Yes." Corinne took it from her bag and gave it to him.

"Oh, one more thing—the covering letter." Bliss got out the old typewriter from the cupboard, inserted the sheet of blank paper to which Banda had appended his new signature, and typed a short, carefully spaced letter to the passport office asking for the application to be handled quickly in view of the short time remaining before the planned date of departure. He then pinned together the forms, the birth certificate, the two photographs, the postal order and the letter, and sealed the package.

"I hope it works," Corinne said. "You seem to me to have taken quite a lot of risks."

"What risks?"

"How do you know you haven't given the real Harold Lever a thirst for travel, with all that talk about the sunny south of France? Suppose he decides to send up for a passport himself? For a coach tour along the Riviera!"

Bliss grimaced. "What a horrible idea!"

"It's possible, isn't it?"

"It's not very likely. People who've been content to stay all their lives in their own country don't usually start traveling abroad at fifty—not without a special reason. He's much more likely to settle for Clacton."

"What would happen if he *did* apply?"

"Well, there'd be a lot of inquiries, of course, and when the facts came out the passport office would obviously cancel the passport that had been issued in his name. But even if Lever did suddenly get a yen for foreign parts, he wouldn't do anything about it yet. He's not free till the end of May. By that time, we'll all be far away. If he ever did get around to it, it might be bad luck for Banda, but the old boy will have to take his chance over that. We're not his keepers for life. Any other bogies?"

"Suppose the passport people check with your bank?"

"They won't do that—they're much too busy. Those chaps are so deep in bumph they can hardly move, especially now, with the Easter holidays coming along. Of course, if they did check we wouldn't get the passport, but that's the worst that could happen. There'd still be no risk. None of this lot can be traced to me. Once I've got rid of the stuff in the deed box, the police could search the house and it wouldn't help them."

"What about the typewriter you've used for all the correspondence?" Corinne said. "Couldn't that give you away?"

Bliss frowned. "H'm—that's a point." He thought for a moment, then smiled. "I know—we'll give it to Oxfam."

Corinne checked the waiter as he prepared once more to fill her glass, and sat back with a contented sigh. "How did you get into this sort of life, Mike?"

They were back at the Gourmet in Frith Street. Bliss, happy to have got the passport application away, had suggested a small celebration lunch to mark their progress to date. Now, with most of the customers gone, they were sipping the last of their wine in a quiet corner and talking about each other. They were both in a state of pleasant euphoria, calm and satisfied in body, serene but lively in mind.

Bliss tapped the ash from his Havana, and grinned. "To tell you the truth, it was all the result of going to Sunday school."

"Don't be absurd."

"Really—I'm not kidding. I was walking to chapel one Sabbath morning and I dropped the penny I'd been given for the collection—down a drain. A man came along and saw me poking about with a stick, looking woebegone, and I told him what had happened, and he gave me another penny."

"I don't see how that would start you on a life of crime."

"You don't? Well, all through prayers I was thinking how easy it had been to acquire that penny, and how I could have got it just as easily if I *hadn't* dropped mine down the drain. The next Saturday I went to the zoo with another boy—we were about ten—and we stopped a man with a kind face and I said I'd lost the return half of my bus ticket. He gave me sixpence. By the end of the afternoon we'd collected five shillings each. That was when I first realized there were a lot of softhearted and unsuspicious people in the world, and that I could tell a convincing story. You could say I never looked back."

"When did you make your first real money?"

"It depends what you mean by real. I pulled off quite a nice little ploy when I was twenty. I was in the lounge bar at London Airport, chatting to an American who was catching a plane home. I was pretending to be from Queensland, just finishing a trip to the Old Country. He asked me why I looked so down in the mouth, and I said I was having to cut the trip short because I was low on cash. He said that was too bad, and I said, yes, it *was* too bad, because I'd just been conned out of twenty pounds. I said some blighter at the hotel where I was staying had told me a tale about having his wallet stolen and I'd been gullible enough to advance him twenty pounds for twenty-four hours and that was the last I'd seen of him. The American reckoned it was a damned shame and insisted on making me a present of twenty pounds before he flew off."

Corinne smiled. "Oh, well, I don't suppose he missed it."

"I'm sure he didn't. He was loaded. A nice guy, and very generous—but why not? I'd be generous if I was stinking rich."

Corinne twiddled the ring on her finger, admiring the stone. "Perhaps you will be, soon."

"With luck, we both will be."

"What will you do with the money, assuming you get it? Buy a vineyard and settle down in the sun?"

"Good lord, no, I like my grapes ready-bottled. I'll probably wander around for a bit—enjoy a Sabbatical —broaden my mind. . . . What about you?"

Corinne shook her head. "I think I'll wait till it happens before I make any plans."

"Still cautious? By the way, what are you going to do about your belongings here? And your flat? Sell up, or hang on?"

"I shall certainly hang on for a bit," Corinne said. "If things don't work out, I might want to come back."

"True. I think I'll hang on, too. After all, we don't have to be here to sell up. I've got a lawyer who'll handle everything for me—chap named Dobson, very reliable. You could use him, too, if you wanted to." Bliss sorted out the change the waiter had brought, leaving a lavish tip.

"So what's the next move?" Corinne asked.

"Well—I think it's about time we got down to working out our schedule for D-day. The movements we'll have to make, who'll do what jobs, departure times and arrangements—all that sort of thing."

Corinne nodded. "It's going to be quite complicated, isn't it?"

"The trickiest part of the whole enterprise. And until we're clear what we want ourselves, we can't tell Kirby what we'd like him to fix. Let's drop in at T. Cook's when we leave here and get some timetables. Then I suggest we go back to the flat and put our heads together. . . ."

"That'll make a change," Corinne said.

By the time they'd made their call and driven back to Hampstead, the lunchtime euphoria was beginning to wear off. Bliss produced a pad and pencil, stacked the timetables beside him, and got quickly down to business.

"It looks," he said, "as though our operation will have to start immediately after the Olsen verdict. Kirby won't want me to leave the country until the trial's over, because witnesses sometimes have to be recalled. And we mustn't seem to be hanging about afterward, because we're supposed to be scared of Olsen's friends."

"I *am* scared," Corinne said. "Remember?"

Bliss smiled indulgently. "Okay, you're scared—but the main thing is it wouldn't *look* good. So D-day will be the day of the verdict. Now there's bound to be a tremendous hue and cry once Banda's disappearance is discovered, so we'll want to get him out of the country as soon as possible after we've snatched him. Before anyone realizes he's gone, if we can."

Corinne nodded. "The same night, in fact."

"Exactly. And that means the schedule's going to be very tight indeed. We won't be able to pick him up at

Lushington before dusk—say around eight-thirty—and
we'll still have to drive to town, get him crated, and
take him on to the terminal. That means a very late
crossing." Bliss paged through his timetables. "There's
a 2:30 a.m. sailing from Dover to Boulogne. We ought
to be able to make that quite comfortably. Or we could
go by air from Lydd to Le Touquet, pretty well any
time. There's a new company that's starting on all-
night service from April onward."

"I'd rather go by sea," Corinne said. "I hate flying."

"Do you? I'm an air man myself, but I don't really
mind either way. So let's say the 2:30 crossing, pro-
visionally. Now about vehicles. We'll have to get some
sort of station wagon or light van for conveying Banda
to the port once he's crated. The chest won't go in an
ordinary car."

"Anyway there'll be our luggage too," Corinne said.
"And don't you think we ought to take a few other
small bits of furniture, so the chest doesn't stand out
too much?"

"Yes—good idea. A light van, then—there'll be more
room in that. And I'd like to take the Mercedes. It's
almost new and I'll drop a hell of a lot on it if I sell
it. Besides, we'll need it in France. So that's two bookings. I suggest you drive the Mercedes to Dover, and
I'll take Banda in the van."

Corinne shook her head. "I'm not going to drive the
Mercedes. Not that night."

"Why ever not?"

"Because Olsen's friends will probably know it's your
car by then. I'm not having anything to do with it."

"Oh, come!" Bliss said. "Surely you're not still worrying about the bomb episode?"

"Not specially that, but if those men are after you, anything could happen. I'm definitely not driving your car."

Bliss shrugged good-humoredly. "Okay, I'll take the Mercedes. Do you mind driving Banda?"

Corinne considered. "No, I don't mind that—not if the van isn't too big. Wait a minute, though—won't it be starting from the flat?"

"Yes, of course."

"Then I'm sorry, but I can't. I'm going to keep right away from here that night. We did agree I wouldn't have to take any risks, and just after the verdict could be the most dangerous time."

"Why?"

"Well, the gang will realize you couldn't get away before and they'll probably expect you to clear off somewhere immediately afterwards. So if they have got it in for you, that's just when they're likely to try something."

Bliss grunted. "M'm—this is a bit awkward. . . . I'm quite sure they won't try anything, you know. It's pure imagination on your part."

"Perhaps it is," Corinne said, "but I'm not taking any chances. Honestly, Mike, this is where I dig my heels in. A bargain's a bargain, and you've got to stick to it."

"I see." Bliss pondered. "Well, I don't know. . . . I can't very well ship the Mercedes beforehand because we're going to need it on D-day. . . ." Suddenly his face cleared. "I've got it! We'll get the police to pick up the van here and take it round to your flat, and you can drive it to Dover from there. And if you're really afraid the Mercedes will be followed, or blown up, or something, I suggest I go by a different route. I'll fly to Le Touquet and we'll meet on the other side. That way, you won't have a thing to worry about."

Corinne looked relieved. "Yes, that's a much better plan."

"It'll impress the police, too, and that's most important. We've got to keep this idea that we're scared right in the forefront of their minds—it's the only thing that makes sense of what we're doing. Good! Now I think we're about ready to do our stuff with Kirby. The sooner he knows what we want, the sooner he can get cracking on the arrangements."

"Will you ask him to come here?"

Bliss nodded. "I'll try to fix something for tomorrow morning."

"Oughtn't I to come along too?"

"I think you should, this time, looking innocent, charming, and as frightened as you like! I'll give you a ring." Bliss's glance rested for a moment on the ring Corinne was wearing. "You'd better switch that big rock to your other hand before you forget or you'll have old Hawkeye wondering."

"Heavens, yes!" Corinne transferred the ring to her left hand. "There. I'm sure no one ever got engaged as cheaply as that before!"

"I wouldn't call it cheap," Bliss said. "It's costing me £112,500!"

The inspector arrived by appointment at eleven o'clock next morning. Bliss received him with what he hoped was an appropriate mixture of gratitude and anxiety.

"I'm so glad you were able to come around, Inspector. Corinne's been getting a bit concerned about the lack of definite arrangements for going away. I guess she's having a slight attack of cold feet. She'll feel better when we've agreed on a plan."

"Well, I'm all set to help, sir."

"Good. I've asked her to join us—she won't be long. . . ." Bliss broke off as he caught the familiar sound of Corinne's Mini below the window. "In fact, here she is. Excuse me." He went to the front door and waited there while Corinne climbed the stairs. "Hullo, darling," he said, in a slightly raised and very affectionate voice. He gave her a smacking kiss. "Come on in, the inspector's here."

Corinne preceded him into the sitting room. She was wearing an apple-green linen dress that matched the bright spring morning, and she looked fresh and charming, and just a little shy. The very picture of a girl in love . . . Her only adornment was the diamond that sparkled convincingly on her engagement finger.

"Darling, this is Inspector Kirby," Bliss said. "Inspector—my fiancée, Corinne Lake." He had no difficulty in sounding proud of her.

Kirby shook hands warmly. "How do you do, Miss Lake. I'm very glad to meet you."

"I'm glad to meet *you*, Inspector—I've heard so much about you. Mike says you've promised to look after us."

"I have indeed," Kirby said.

"It's been so worrying. I expect Mike told you—we talked about it for ages before he decided. About giving evidence, I mean. I feel horribly frightened, but we just didn't see what else we could do—not and keep our self-respect."

Kirby gave her an approving smile. "I think you've faced up to your responsibilities with great courage, Miss Lake. As I told Mr. Bliss, I don't believe there's any danger to speak of, but I know that thinking there may be can be almost as bad. Anyhow, you can depend on me."

"Thank you, Inspector. I'm sure we can."

"Right," Bliss said, "let's get to work, shall we? We've a lot of ground to cover." Corinne sat down, and the two men resumed their seats. "I've made a few notes, Inspector, so we won't overlook anything. First, about our belongings. There'll be no problem for you there. As far as the bulk of our things is concerned, we both think the simplest course is to sell up and start again jointly in France. We'll arrange that by post when we're safely on the other side. We don't want furniture movers around while we're still here, drawing attention to the fact that we're going. So that leaves us with only a few minor things to transport. Our personal effects, of course. A few books that we don't want to part with. We can pack those in suitcases. Then Corinne would like to take a small table."

"It's a little Queen Anne table," Corinne said. "I couldn't bear to leave it behind."

"And I've got an oak chest I'd like to hang on to. It's not much to look at but it's been in the family for a long time. Oh, and four dozen bottles of Romanée Conti that my godfather gave me. I can pack those in the chest. Sounds like coals to Newcastle, I know, but it isn't really."

"Another special vintage, Mr. Bliss?"

"Out of this world, Inspector. A masterpiece—and quite irreplaceable. By the way, darling, remind me we'll need some straw for packing the bottles. . . . And that's about all, apart from a few oddments. We thought if we could get hold of a small van we could easily take everything with us."

"No trouble at all, I should think," Kirby said.

"Right—then that's what we'll do. Now, could you get the van for us, Inspector, and see to the necessary paper work? License, insurance and so forth? I'll foot the bill, of course. The thing is, I want to have as little to do with these preliminary arrangements as possible. That way there'll be less chance of leaving a trail."

"Yes, I can do that," Kirby said. "Have you any particular sort of van in mind?"

"Not really. I should think one of those small Bedfords would be about the job. It needn't be new, as long as it's in good running order."

"Very well, sir, I'll attend to it. Would you like us to keep it till it's wanted?"

"If you don't mind. I've no garage, and a van parked outside the house might attract attention. Right, that's that. Now we come to the travel arrangements, and here there's a bit of a complication." Bliss told the inspector of Corinne's fears about the Mercedes, of her anxiety to keep away from the flat on the day of departure, and of their consequent decision to travel separately. This, Bliss realized, was a slightly awkward corner. Most loving couples, soon to be married, would prefer to face any danger together. And he was supposed to be as scared as Corinne, so he mustn't seem too happy about the arrangement. "I guess I'm cast for the role of decoy," he said, with a wry shrug. "Anyway, it's obviously better for one of us to take a chance

than for two, and it is my responsibility. I'll just have
to be very careful."

Kirby gave a tolerant smile. "Well, I'm sure there's
no *need* for any of this. It's not at all likely that anyone will interfere with your car or follow you—and I
shall station a man outside the flat when the time
comes, to make sure there's no trouble there."

"All the same," Corinne said, wrinkling her forehead
in an attractive frown, "I know I'd feel like a jelly if I
had to be around. You must think me an awful coward,
Inspector—especially as Mike will have to take the risk
anyway—but I honestly don't believe I could face it."

"I certainly don't think you're a coward," Kirby said.
"Very much the reverse. And if you're going to feel
happier keeping right out of the way, that's obviously
the sensible thing to do. . . . So what exactly is your
plan, Mr. Bliss?"

Bliss breathed again. They'd rounded the dangerous
corner. Kirby was evidently prepared to humor them
about everything.

"Well," he said, "first there's the question of when
we'll go. I assume we shan't be able to leave until the
trial's over in case I'm still needed, but we'd like to
get away as soon after the verdict as possible. Prefera-
bly the same day."

Kirby nodded. "That should be all right."

"Good. Now we'll still be in some hideaway hotel
in the country, of course, and we may not get the verdict till the end of the day, so it'll mean late crossings.
My idea is that we should drive up to London in the
evening—after dark, for safety's sake, and separately,
because we'll have two cars—and do our packing in

our respective flats, and then cross to France during the night. Corinne will take the 2:30 a.m. car ferry to Boulogne, and I'll fly to Le Touquet around 2:00. If you could have one of your chaps bring the van round here, say at 11:30, and help to load it up, and then drive it to Corinne's place at Knightsbridge, she could take over from there with an easy mind. How's that?"

"Whatever you say, Mr. Bliss. It's entirely up to you. I'll arrange that with pleasure."

"Splendid. And could you get the tickets for us, as discreetly as possible? Again, I'm most anxious that we shouldn't get involved in the preliminaries ourselves. I want as few people as possible to know we're leaving."

"I understand, sir. Yes, I'll get the tickets for you. I shan't be able to make firm bookings, of course, till much nearer the time, because we won't know the date, but if I have a quiet word with the carriers I expect they'll make an effort to fit you in at short notice."

"That's what I thought," Bliss said. "Which they probably wouldn't do for me. Then there's the question of customs clearance for the van and its contents, and for the Mercedes, export and import licenses—you probably know about these things . . ."

"*I* don't, but I'll find someone who does. I'll attend to it."

"And will you do your best to smooth the way at the ports? I don't want any hitches or delays on either side of the Channel."

"Leave it to me, Mr. Bliss. I'll drop a word in the right quarter and you'll both get VIP treatment all the way."

Bliss smiled encouragingly at Corinne. "No one

could say fairer than that, eh, darling? Cheer up—everything's going to be all right."

"I expect it is," Corinne said. "But I'll be thankful when we're safely in Provence, all the same."

"I'm with you there," Bliss said. "Roll on the day!" He glanced once more at his notes. "Last but not least, Inspector, there's the money problem. I'll need to transfer about £5,000 to France—maybe more later, but that'll do for a start. And we'll need some traveler's checks for the journey—more than the usual allowance. Could you put in a tactful word with the Bank of England, so there's no holdup?"

Kirby nodded. "When they know of the special circumstances, I'm sure there'll be no difficulty."

"Fine. Well, I think that's about all at the moment. We'll have plenty of time to deal with any small matters that crop up. . . . Anything on *your* mind, darling?"

Corinne shook her head. "It all sounds very satisfactory. What a thing it is to have a friend in court!"

Kirby got to his feet. "I'm only too happy to oblige, Miss Lake."

"I'm afraid we're giving you a great deal of trouble, all the same," Bliss said. "You probably think we're being absurdly fussy, but there is a lot at stake for us. We don't want to have to spend the rest of our lives looking over our shoulders."

"It won't be any trouble at all, sir," Kirby said cheerfully. "Compared with some of the jobs we have to do, handling these small matters will be a rest cure."

"I suppose so. How's the case going, by the way?"

"The committal proceedings will be in about ten days' time. I'll be in touch with you before then, of

course, about the arrangements. The trial should follow quite soon after that." Kirby held out his hand to
Corinne. "Good-bye, Miss Lake. If I may say so, I can
quite understand why Mr. Bliss is so anxious to take
care of you."

Corinne gave him a sweet smile. "Thank you, Inspector—that's very nice of you. And thank you for
being so sympathetic and helpful. I feel so much happier now."

"I'm very glad. I can assure you there's absolutely
no need to worry. I'll see you get safely to Provence.
Good-bye for now, Mr. Bliss." The inspector nodded,
and went briskly out.

As the door closed behind him, Bliss looked at Corinne and drew a long breath. "Well, I'm glad that's
over," he said. "A pretty sticky interview. I don't know
about you, my love, but I could use a reviver."

A short period of marking time followed their meeting with Kirby. Nothing more could be done to advance the plot until Harold Lever's passport arrived,
which Bliss didn't expect to happen for at least a week.
All the same, he began to keep a close eye on the hall
table again. Each morning, after the postman had
come, he descended to the first-floor landing and
glanced over the banisters to see if there was an
official-looking envelope of the right size and shape
among the letters.

On the fifth morning, to his gratified surprise, there
was. A squarish, grayish envelope, promisingly plump.
Bliss approached it with caution. If, by any remote
chance, the authorities *had* checked the application
with the bank, they could have sent the envelope as a

bait. There could be police watchers around. He passed the table, went out to his car, took a package of cigarettes from the glove box, and glanced casually up and down the road as he lit one. No watchers! He returned to the hall. No footsteps on the stairs. No doors opening. All quite safe. And the envelope, he saw, *was* for Harold Lever.

Humming softly to himself—"Onward, Christian Soldiers"—he carried the passport upstairs. For once, even he could find no fault with the functioning of the bureaucratic machine. It had worked with speed and efficiency, and apart from issuing a brand-new passport to a composite man with a criminal record, it had made not a single mistake. As he leafed through the crisp and virgin pages in the privacy of his study, pausing at the photograph he'd taken, the bogus signature he'd watched being penned, he felt a deep glow of pride in his technical achievement. Not one man in a hundred thousand could have pulled it off. Confidence bubbled up in him. The way was clear now for the next big push, and all the signs were favorable. He could hardly wait to get started.

First, though, he must do a bit of tidying up. Get rid of the evidence. The official envelope. The leaflet of instructions. The birth certificate that the passport office had returned. He wouldn't be needing that any more. And the negative of the photograph, which he'd kept as a precaution—that could go now, too. He tore the certificate and envelope and leaflet into small pieces and flushed them away. Splendid thing, he thought, modern plumbing. Then he burned the negative in an ash tray.

On his way to the wastebin with the charred remains, he glanced at the barometer in the hall. It was
high, and when he tapped the face the pointer went
even higher. No need for a special weather forecast
this time. The day was set fair.

He changed into his dark clothes and soft-soled
shoes. Then he telephoned Corinne. He spoke with
studied vagueness, though the risk of being overheard
was slight. The package they'd been expecting had
arrived, he said. Everything was in order, and he was
going down to the country right away. He'd be making final arrangements with their client that evening,
and he'd be getting in touch with her as soon as he
returned.

By the early afternoon he was once more on his way
to Sussex, with Harold Lever's passport tucked snugly
in his breast pocket.

To start with, the operation went as smoothly as it
had done on the first occasion. Bliss telephoned from
Lushington precisely at seven-fifteen and got through
to Banda without difficulty. The silent message was
conveyed. The short trip to the copse through the
gathering dusk passed without incident. Everything
seemed set. It wasn't until Bliss turned the Mercedes
into the trees that his headlights showed he had an
unforeseen problem on his hands. A car was already
parked there, and a man and a girl were amorously
engaged on the back seat.

Bliss switched off his lights and considered his op-
tions. The gate he had to climb was close to the parked
car—too close to be used with safety, under the eyes
of the couple. There might be a gap in the hedge

higher up the road, but the hedge was a good one, and the gap was a gamble. If he drove on past the house and tried to approach it on foot from the other direction, he would have to pass the guard car to reach the culvert. Of course, he could abandon the visit and try again some other night. He wasn't tied to this particular night. But Banda would soon be out there for the second time, chatting away to the policeman in the dark. A third time might begin to look odd. Also, it would be bad for morale.

Bliss glanced at his watch. He had, perhaps, twenty minutes in hand before he had to start his trek up the field—twenty minutes to break up the amorous pair. It was worth a try, even at the risk of a punch-up. Better than retreat. He drove a little farther into the copse and switched on his headlights again. The beam wasn't directly on the parked car, but it was near enough to illuminate the interior. He lit a cigarette, and waited.

The man and the girl had disengaged. Bliss could see them staring back through their rear window. The girl began to tidy her hair. Presently the door opened and the man got out. He wasn't, Bliss was relieved to see, a very big man. He took a step or two toward the Mercedes, then turned and said something to the girl through the open door. The girl got out, smoothing her dress. Both of them changed to the front seats. The car's lights went on. The engine started. The car began to reverse out. As it shaved past the Mercedes, the man shouted something. It sounded like "Nosy bastard!" In a moment it had roared away up the road and Bliss had the copse to himself.

There were no more hitches. Bliss found his transit of the fields much more straightforward on this second occasion, and his progress was rapid. The clear, fine night, though it added slightly to the chance of being seen, also made it easier for him to pick his way beside the hedge. Nor, this time, was he encumbered by the attaché case. In a few minutes he had reached the culvert and passed through to the grassy bank. Banda had remembered the drill and was already chatting to the guard—almost at the far end of the garden, judging by the low rumble of their voices. There'd be no risk of interception tonight. By twenty past eight Bliss was safely through the French doors sitting in the study behind drawn curtains waiting for Banda to appear.

There were the same noises as before—the slam of the front door, the heavy tread in the passage. Bliss murmured his quiet "Okay" as the study door opened. The light clicked on. For a moment the two men regarded each other. Then, with a slightly theatrical gesture, Bliss whipped the passport from his pocket and held it out. "There you are!" he said, smiling. "All orders promptly executed."

Banda took the passport, looked at the photograph, turned the pages. The effect the little blue book had on him was striking. Hitherto he had been an interested but openly skeptical observer of Bliss's activities. Now, plainly, he was more impressed. "Remarkable!" he said. "Quite remarkable!"

Bliss gave a modest shrug. "Not really—just a routine part of the Bliss service. Competent, of course. When you get to France you can have your hair cut short and darkened a bit. Once that's done, and you've grown your mustache, you'll be able to get by with that passport anywhere."

Banda was still staring at the photograph. "Yes. With this, I really believe I could get to South America."

"I'm glad you're satisfied," Bliss said. "So does that mean we go ahead with the plan?"

Banda sank into a chair. "It means we talk about it. . . . If I am now to take this enterprise seriously, there are many questions I must ask you."

"Well, now is the time. Ask away!"

"The first is the most important of all. You have not told me yet how you propose to get me away from here."

"I shall stage a car crash," Bliss said. "Close to the house, so that it will draw the guards off. In the confusion, you'll be able to leave without any trouble. You'll be picked up by Corinne a hundred yards down the road, and driven away. There'll be no problem at all."

Banda looked unconvinced. "As usual, you make things sound very simple. Will it not, in fact, be rather difficult to stage this crash?"

"It won't be nearly as difficult as it was to get the passport," Bliss said. "Don't worry—I've got all the details worked out. You can safely leave it to me."

"Suppose the guards do not behave as you expect when the crash occurs?"

"They will," Bliss said. "It simply isn't in a policeman's nature not to rush to the spot when there's a bad smash right on their doorstep."

"But afterward—what if they become suspicious and call at the house? What if they discover I have gone? There will be a chase, perhaps road blocks."

"If you leave your bedroom light on behind drawn curtains," Bliss said, "and your bedroom television set working, they won't become suspicious and they won't discover you've gone—probably not till morning. They'll simply assume you've retired early to watch the programs in comfort. It won't be the first time you've done it, so they won't be surprised. Anyway, they'll be so busy searching for a nonexistent body after the crash they won't have time to bother about you. As long as they can see your light they'll be quite satisfied."

"Will they not be surprised that I do not notice the crash myself, and come out?"

"Not if the telly's on loud. And not if you've been pretending to be deaf, as I told you to."

"Ah—so that was the reason." Banda paused. "Suppose they wish to use my telephone to report the car crash?"

"They won't do that. They've got their own radio cars."

"Suppose my telephone rings after I have gone, and no one answers it? Will they not think it strange? Will they not investigate?"

"Before you leave," Bliss said, "you'll pull the wire from the socket. Then it won't ring."

Banda grunted. "Well—your plan *might* work, I suppose."

"It will work—you'll see. Right—next question!"

"How big is this chest that I am supposed to travel in?"

"About the size of a coffin!" Bliss said, with a grin. "But there's plenty of room for you, both ways. I've measured it. You'll be quite comfortable."

"How will you convey it?"

"In a small van, with our personal belongings. The van's already laid on."

"How long will I have to remain in it?"

"If things go according to plan, I'd say about five or six hours."

"How will I breathe?"

"There's a wide crack in the lid that'll let in all the air you'll need."

"Suppose I am attacked by claustrophobia? Suppose I require to get out in some emergency? I do not relish the prospect of being locked into a chest that I cannot open."

"You won't be," Bliss said. "The chest has an outside lock, but I shall only pretend to turn it. I'll fix a catch inside, which you'll be able to operate yourself."

"Ah—that is better." Banda sat in thought for a moment. "How will you account for the weight?"

"The chest will theoretically contain bottles." Bliss told Banda about the Romanée Conti. "Four dozen bottles would weigh just about the same as you do. So the weight won't cause any surprise."

"H'm. You will have to make sure, my friend, that no one sees the actual bottles after we have left. Otherwise they will know there has been a deception."

"No one will see them," Bliss said, "for the simple reason that I haven't got them. They're just a figment. If I'd been the happy possessor of four dozen bottles of glorious Romanée Conti, you can bet your life I'd have swigged the lot long ago."

"I see. But . . ." Banda looked puzzled. "What I do not understand is why it was necessary to make up this story about the wine. Would it not have been simpler to say you were packing the chest with books? They, too, would have been heavy."

"I know," Bliss said, "but there's more to it than weight. I had to think how to give you a smooth, safe trip. If the chest got thrown about during loading, you could be hurt; you might cry out and give the show away. The only way to insure careful handling is to put labels on the chest—'Glass With Care'—that sort of thing. And the labels have to be justified by the known contents. So, incidentally, does the packing I shall need to use to make you comfortable. The police will see traces of straw in the room. Hence the story about the wine."

Banda nodded slowly. "Yes, that is sensible. Sensible and convincing. You think of everything."

Bliss grinned. "Let's hope you're right!"

There was a short silence. Then Banda resumed his probing. "When is this attempt to be made?"

"I'd guess in about four or five weeks. Perhaps a bit less. We shall be leaving on the night of the day the trial of Jack Olsen ends. He's the man I'm giving evidence against—the man who was responsible for the shooting at the Queen of Hearts Club. I'm sure you've read about the case."

"I have read about the shooting, yes."

"Well, when the trial starts you must follow its progress on the radio—all the time. On the last day, you'll hear the verdict on the six o'clock news. That'll be your green light. By eight forty-five you must be ready to leave the house. Around that time I shall organize the car crash. You'll hear it when it happens—I'll make sure of that! The guards will rush to the scene. You'll watch them go. As soon as the coast's clear you'll creep through the culvert and make your way down two fields to the copse of beech trees on the left. Corinne will be waiting there with her car, and she'll drive you to London."

Banda nodded. "Then what do I do?"

Bliss took a piece of paper from Banda's desk and drew a sketch map. "This is Bampton Gardens, where I live. Number 15. My flat is number 10, on the top floor. Now this is Cranford Gardens, a parallel road that runs behind it. Corinne will drop you at the corner of Cranford Gardens—here. She won't want to go any nearer because she's scared of Olsen's gang. She's got a daft idea they might be watching out for me. Anyway, they won't be watching out for you! You'll walk down Cranford Gardens until you come to a bright green gate on the left with number 15 on it. The gate leads into the back garden of my house. You'll make sure there's no one around in the road, then you'll go into the garden. Ahead of you, you'll see a spiral fire escape. You'll climb to the top window, which will appear to be shut but which in fact will be unfastened. You'll push up the window, climb in, shut it behind you, and stay there in the dark until I arrive, which should be about fifteen minutes later. That's all you have to do. I'll deal with everything else when I get there."

Banda frowned down at the paper. "This climbing of the fire escape—is that not going to be more dangerous than if I went boldly through the front door and let myself into your flat with a key?"

"No," Bliss said, "because there'll probably be a plain-clothes policeman on watch at the front of the house."

"I see. . . . But suppose someone notices me during these acrobatics?"

"No one will," Bliss said. "There are only two windows below mine that open on the fire escape, and they're windows of back rooms that are hardly ever used. And no one ever goes into the garden at night. Of course, if by any chance you are noticed, and challenged, you'll just have to use your loaf—say you're a house guest of mine, and you've left your key in the flat. People are very simple, you know. You can bluff your way through anything."

"My experience has been different," Banda said ruefully. "However, I will do my best. And after you join me—what will happen then?"

"I shall pack you up in the chest, the police will remove you to the van and drive you to Knightsbridge and Corinne will take you on from there. The actual arrangements needn't concern you. They're in the safe hands of Inspector Kirby of the C.I.D., a most efficient officer! Now—any more questions?"

"No, I think not."

"Then this is the moment of decision. I've produced the passport as I promised, and I've outlined the plan. Can I take it that you're prepared to go ahead?"

"Well . . ." Banda wiped a few drops of sweat from his forehead. "Yes, I suppose so."

"On my terms? Two hundred thousand when you're free in France? And no tricks?"

"The figure is extortionate, but—yes. I am in no position to argue."

"You *are* in a position to pay, though?"

"As it happens, I am."

"In that case, I'll be glad to have the deposit. How are you going to arrange the transfer?"

Banda moved to his desk and took up a pen. "I will

write a letter to my bank in Zurich, which you can post. Mine is a numbered account. There will be no trouble. What instructions do you wish me to give?"

Bliss dictated. "Please transfer £25,000 from my account to the credit of Mr. Michael Bliss at the Crédit Lyonnais, 4 Rue Foch, Aix-en-Provence."

"They know you there?"

"Yes, I keep a small balance with them."

"That is convenient." Banda completed the letter. "Do you wish to see what I have written?"

Bliss shook his head. "If the money doesn't come through, you won't go through either. So I guess I can trust you."

Banda found an envelope and addressed it. "And I, of course, am trusting you, my friend. I am about to pay you £25,000 for a passport that I may not be able to use. How do I know I shall ever hear from you again? How do I know that this is not the end of your plan? You are, after all, a self-confessed confidence man."

Bliss chuckled. "It's a nice thought, but you really don't have to worry. When the roll is called up yonder I'll be there. This deposit is only the hors d'oeuvres. It's the meal I'm interested in."

"Well, that is a persuasive answer. Let us hope your meal will not prove too indigestible!" Banda handed over the letter, which Bliss put in his pocket.

"Right," Bliss said. "I think that about finishes our business. You've got your instructions, you know what to do. Now it's up to you to make a good job of it." He glanced around the study, mentally tidying up. "If you're going to keep that sketch plan you'd better lock it away safely, so your woman doesn't see it. Your passport, too, of course. And whatever you do, don't forget to bring the passport with you on departure night."

"The passport, the mustache, the glasses and the gum—I shall remember. What about clothes? Luggage?"

"Come in what you stand up in. Light clothes, no overcoat, no luggage. We'll fix you up with everything you need."

"Very well. Shall I be seeing you again before then?"

"I wouldn't think so. If any emergency arises, anything to change the plan, you'll know on the night because there'll be no car crash. In that case you'll wait until I get in touch with you again, in the usual way. But I don't expect any crises."

"Suppose something happens to me? Suppose I fall ill?"

"You'll have to make it somehow," Bliss said grimly, "even if it means crawling down the field on your hands and knees! Once that car has crashed, there'll be no second chance for you. And there's no way you can safely get in touch with me. So don't fall ill!"

Banda sighed. "Well, we must hope for the best." He was silent for a moment, gazing down at the floor. "We must hope, too, that your plan comes off. I am still not confident. It is a very audacious plan, Mr. Bliss."

"Exactly," Bliss agreed. *"Toujours l'audace!*—as we'll soon be saying. That's why it's going to work."

They followed the same procedure as before for getting Bliss away. Banda went upstairs and turned on the radio. The sound of music swelled through the house. Bliss opened one of the French doors, cautiously, and peered out through the gap.

What he saw gave him a nasty shock. The night had become much brighter. The edge of a big moon was just beginning to show above a belt of trees. That was something he hadn't taken into account.

He hesitated, but only for a second. To send Banda out for another chat so soon after the first would be asking for trouble, and anyway, by the time the move had been organized the whole moon would be up. Better to take a chance now, before the garden became bathed in light.

Bliss eased himself through the door, pushed it to, and quickly rounded the corner of the house, keeping close to the wall. As the music behind him grew fainter, another sound became audible—the guard walking in the road beyond the hedge. Some yards away—but walking in Bliss's direction. At any moment he'd be able to see over the wooden gate. Bliss made a dive for the grassy bank. He was almost down when a piece of rock, dislodged by his foot, went clattering to the bed of the stream, hitting the side of the culvert with a sharp crack.

Bliss ducked into the culvert and waited there, bent low, listening. He could hear the guard's footsteps approaching the bridge. Suddenly a light flashed on. A torch beam, directed over the parapet, straight down to the bed of the stream. It stayed for a moment, then clicked off. Footsteps again, just overhead. Not receding. What was the guard doing? Crossing the road? Silence, now. Had he stopped? Or had he gone into the field? Bliss's pulse raced. A wrong decision now, and the game would be up before it had started.

Should he go on through the culvert or back to the stream bed? Or just stay put? Back, he thought. He stepped out from under the low roof, away from the opening. Almost at once, a beam of light was directed through the culvert from the field end. Another second, and he'd have been caught in it!

He waited, tensely, strained against the wall of the bridge, trying to pick out telltale sounds above the distant music. Suddenly the radio went off. A dry stick crackled at the far end of the culvert. Was the guard coming through . . . ? No . . . the stick must have been in the field . . . Now footsteps overhead again. Crossing the road . . . Bliss plunged into the culvert, padded through, and listened again at the field end. Footsteps receding now. Unhurried, rhythmic. The guard had satisfied himself. It had been a damned near thing, but the flap was over.

Bliss waited till the guard was safely out of sight and earshot, then made his way quickly down the two fields. He was humming softly to himself as he approached the Mercedes—an old Moody and Sankey tune. "Count Your Blessings."

III

"CALL MICHAEL BLISS!"

Bliss pushed through the swing doors of the court-room and walked—not too slowly, not too briskly—toward the witness box. The moment had come to pay off the first installment of his prospective debt to the police; to earn their gratitude—and he intended to make a thorough job of it. The conscientious citizen doing his duty—that was the role today. The bystander who hadn't just stood by. It was an easier role than most, because for once he was actually going to tell the truth. There shouldn't be any surprises. He'd been over the ground with the prosecution and was well briefed on what was likely to happen. All he had to do was strike the right note, the one that would convince the magistrate he was a sound and reliable witness. He mustn't be too confident, too eager, as though he had some ax to grind. He mustn't allow himself to be needled or confused by the defense. He must be thoughtful in his manner, quietly firm in his replies. He'd got it all worked out.

He entered the box. The man with the Bible in his hand was momentarily engaged. Bliss glanced around

the court. He'd never been in a police court before.
Pretty austere place, with so much bare wood. . . .
Bench, clerks, lawyers . . . Jack Olsen in the dock,
writing something on a pad . . . Two policemen standing beside him . . . A scattering of the public in rows
of seats at the back . . . Some of them fairly tough-
looking customers—friends of the prisoner, no doubt.
Bliss reflected that he might usefully mention them to
Kirby after the hearing. It would help to strengthen
the act.

The usher was ready now. "Take the book in your
right hand. . . ." Bliss repeated the oath in a low, clear
voice.

Prosecuting counsel rose and addressed him. "You
are Michael Bliss of 15 Bampton Gardens, London, and
you are a free-lance journalist?"

"Yes."

"Did you, on the night of March 3rd last, visit the
Queen of Hearts Club in Avery Street, Park Lane?"

"I did."

"What time did you leave the premises?"

"About two o'clock in the morning."

"Will you please tell the court in your own words
what you did and what you saw around that time?"

Bliss told of his walk to the mews, of sitting in his
car without lights while he felt for a cigarette, of the
second car that had drawn up, of the man with the
gun, and of the shots that had followed when the car
drove away.

Prosecuting counsel gave an approving nod. "What
was this man doing when you first saw him?"

"He was leaning out of the offside front window,
looking ahead."

"Was the offside of the car the side nearest to you?"

"Yes."

"Was the window right down or only partly down?"

"It was right down."

"Did you see the man's face clearly before he covered it?"

"Yes."

"In profile, or full face?"

"Both."

"How would you describe the lighting in the street at the time?"

"It was good. There was a street lamp at the corner of the mews."

"Thank you. Now would you kindly look round the court, Mr. Bliss. Can you see among those present the man who held the gun?"

"Yes."

"Please point him out."

Bliss looked at Olsen. Olsen stared back at him, his pale eyes as friendly as a rattlesnake's.

Bliss pointed. "That's the man—the man in the dock."

Counsel nodded. "Now did you, on March 6th, attend an identification parade at Gerald Street police station?"

"I did."

"And did you on that occasion identify a man as the gunman?"

"Yes."

"The man who is now the prisoner?"

"Yes."

"Did you feel any doubt or hesitancy about the identification?"

"None whatever."

"You recognized the man the moment you saw him?"

"Yes."

"And you're still quite certain the prisoner is the man you saw with the gun?"

"Absolutely positive."

"Thank you."

Prosecuting counsel sat. Defense counsel rose. His approach to Bliss was courteous and a little wary.

"Would you mind telling me, Mr. Bliss, how long you have been a member of the Queen of Hearts Club?"

"About a month."

"This was not your first visit, I take it?"

"No—my second."

"Your second . . . Are you fond of gambling?"

"Not particularly."

"Then why did you join the Club?"

"I wanted to collect material for an article I was planning on 'Gambling in London.'"

"I see. . . ." Counsel looked slightly put out. "Did you write the article?"

"Yes. I sent it to the *Sunday Recorder*."

"Has it been accepted?"

"Not yet, but I hope it may be."

"Did you gamble at all while you were at the club?"

"Yes, I played roulette for a while."

"Strictly in the line of duty?"

Bliss permitted himself a faint smile. "Not entirely. I thought that while I was there I might as well have a flutter."

"Did you win?"

"No, I lost."

"How much did you lose?"

"About a hundred pounds."

"Really! And how much will you get for the article, if it's accepted?"

"Perhaps—twenty-five guineas."

"An expensive evening!"

Bliss nodded. "Fortunately I have private means. I write mainly as a hobby."

"I see." Counsel abandoned his line of questioning, having got less than nowhere. "Well, now, Mr. Bliss, I'd like you to cast your mind back to the time when you were sitting in your car in the mews. How far would you say you were from the man with the gun?"

Bliss considered. "I would say—twenty to thirty feet."

"As much as that? And how long was the gunman's face exposed to you before he covered the lower part of it?"

Again, Bliss took his time. "Two or three seconds."

"Two or three seconds . . . And at that distance, in that short time, by the light of a street lamp, you were really able to register a firm impression of a face?"

"Certainly."

"Don't you think that remarkable?"

"Not at all. The eye is a camera. A split second is enough."

"A camera records on a film, Mr. Bliss."

"The eye records on the brain, sir. I have an exact impression of the face I saw."

"You mean you think you have. Very well." Counsel resumed his seat.

There followed the tedious business of reading over the evidence that Bliss had given and getting the approval of the deposition. Then he was released.

He walked slowly back toward the swing doors, his progress followed by a scowling Olsen. As he passed the public seats, he half expected to meet more hostile glances from the men he'd thought were Olsen's friends, but no one took much notice of him. At close quarters they looked more severe than tough. More like ordinary citizens, taking a grave view of a gangster's activities. But Kirby wouldn't know that. They'd be worth a mention.

A friendly plain-clothes policeman attached himself to Bliss outside the courtroom. "There's a private office where you can wait until the hearing's over, sir. Would you care to follow me?"

"I'd be glad to." Bliss glanced up and down the corridor, registering uneasiness. "I feel a bit exposed now they all know who I am."

The policeman nodded. "Inspector Kirby thought you might like a bit of company." He led the way into a small room, minimally furnished. "Not exactly the Ritz, sir, but I don't think the Inspector will be long. I'm told the defense aren't calling any witnesses."

Bliss took a chair and settled down to wait. For twenty minutes he chatted amiably with the policeman—about the case, about gambling clubs, about the policeman's experiences. Then Kirby joined them. He was beaming.

"Congratulations, Mr. Bliss! You did very well indeed. A splendid witness."

"Thank you. Has Olsen been committed?"

"He certainly has. With your evidence, there was never a doubt of it."

"What was the defense counsel getting at? Asking me all those questions about the Club?"

"He was just probing, sir. Hoping to discover you were an inveterate gambler, I imagine—not to be trusted. But you dealt with him more than adequately."

Bliss gave a faint shrug. "There's really no problem when you're telling the truth. What happened before I came in? About the alibi?"

"Oh, they're in a tough spot over that. I gave evidence about the initial statement Olsen made, and about my discoveries at the house on the river, and they didn't cross-examine. Probably they haven't decided yet what line to take. They reserved their defense, of course. . . . But there's nothing to worry about. I'm sure Olsen will be convicted."

Bliss grunted. "There were some pretty hostile types in that court—in the public seats. Buddies of Olsen, I should think."

"Really, sir? I didn't see any faces I knew."

"Well, as I passed I'm sure I heard someone say, 'We'll get you!' It was only a murmur, but it registered all right!"

"H'm. You've no idea who said it?"

"No—it was from somewhere behind me. It could have been anyone."

"I see. Well, I shouldn't let it upset you, sir. No one's likely to follow it up. There's a lot of difference between a verbal threat and action."

"I hope you're right, Inspector. All the same, I'll feel happier when I'm out of London. Are we ready to go?"

"Yes, sir, everything's laid on. Did you get your hotel fixed up?"

Bliss nodded. "We're staying at an inn called the Blue Boar, just off the Eastbourne road near Lewes. Corinne's already there. I drove my car down yesterday, and I'm booked in as Henry Freeman. I hope I don't forget the name—I'm not used to aliases."

Kirby smiled. "You won't forget it. It's a good, simple name. By the way, do you want anything done about your mail while you're in the country?"

"Oh, yes—please. Could someone collect it from Bampton Gardens? The letters are always left on the table in the front hall."

"Very well. I'll have a man look in every couple of days or so. We'll put any letters in a fresh envelope and post them to Henry Freeman at the Blue Boar. All right?"

"Splendid," Bliss said.

"And if there's anything else, don't hesitate to ring me at the Yard. Okay, sir, if you'll follow me . . ."

Kirby led the way through a maze of corridors, with Bliss close behind him and the plain-clothes man bringing up the rear. They emerged into the street through a side door. A gray Riley saloon was parked at the curb, with another plain-clothes man at the wheel. Kirby gave a casual glance to right and left, opened the passenger door beside the driver, and helped Bliss in. Then he and the first man got into the back and the car drove quickly away.

Kirby turned once or twice to look through the rear window at following traffic. "Seems all right," he said, "but we'll make quite sure. I've arranged for a transfer."

In five minutes they were at Scotland Yard. A blue Ford Cortina was waiting in the courtyard. The Riley drew up alongside it and Kirby shepherded Bliss into the Ford. "The driver will look after you now, sir," he said. "I'll be in touch with you by telephone. My regards to Miss Lake." He raised his hand in salute, and the car shot away.

Bliss was very cheerful and relaxed that evening. In prospect, his court appearance had seemed a bit of an ordeal, but now it was just another success to look back on, another small triumph in the battle of wits, which he took pleasure in telling Corinne about. He particularly enjoyed describing the discomfiture of defense counsel over the newspaper article. Those innocent-sounding questions about his gambling activities might have reduced his status as a witness quite appreciably if he hadn't already prepared his cover story and actually written and sent off the article. But because of his foresight, everything had gone splendidly. With Olsen safely committed and an early conviction likely, he was more than ever Kirby's blue-eyed boy. The outlook couldn't have been brighter.

Corinne was cheerful, too. Now that they were tucked away in the country, her fears about the gang were temporarily lulled. She was satisfied, from what Mike had said, that he hadn't been followed from London. No newspaper had been able to photograph him, so it was most unlikely that anyone would recognize him in Sussex. As Henry Freeman he would arouse no curiosity even among people who were following the case closely. And the gang hadn't had a chance yet to become interested in the Mercedes. For the moment, there was no danger at all.

Both of them were pleased with their choice of an

inn. The Blue Boar was small but very comfortable, and they had two delightful rooms looking out over the Downs. The inn was well situated for shopping and cinema visits and restaurant meals in Eastbourne or Brighton, and as it was only ten miles or so from Max Banda's house it would make a very convenient takeoff point when the moment came. They had two cars for running around in, and a lovely countryside to explore in weather that was exceptionally fine. They could settle down, as Bliss said, in peace and seclusion, to enjoy a quiet holiday and perfect their plans.

It was to their plans that Bliss returned as they sat in the bar that evening, enjoying a Martini before dinner. "You know," he said, "I think it's time we made that list we've been talking about. Things to get and things to do. Otherwise we may overlook something vital."

He fetched a piece of paper from the writing room and drew his chair closer to Corinne's, so they could talk quietly. "Now let's see. First of all—wine racks."

"That's a new one," Corinne said. "Why wine racks?"

"Just in case old Hawkeye shows up at the flat on departure night and happens to see into the glory hole. No one would keep bottles of good wine standing upright or rolling about on the floor, and Kirby would probably know that. He'd expect to see empty racks when the chest's closed up. We can't be too careful with that fellow—he's got a dangerously split mind. Talks about one thing while he's concentrating on another. Very crafty."

Corinne smiled. "All right—wine racks."

"Then we'll need to get some sort of catch to fix on the inside of the chest. Banda's scared to death of being locked in. I think he imagines that boat sinking under him. Oh, and a bale of straw for packing. I don't know where we'll get that—some farm, perhaps."

"And labels for the chest," Corinne said.

"Yes. Any good stationer's for those, I should think. And a large box of matches—one of those jumbo boxes one sees around."

"What do you want the matches for?"

Bliss grinned. "Arson, dear! Now let's see—we must think about Banda's comfort on the journey. Give him good value for his two hundred thou.! He'd better have a proper water bottle in the chest. It'll be easier to drink from than an ordinary bottle. And something to sustain him in case he gets hungry—chocolate, perhaps. And some seasickness pills in case the weather's bad."

"Did you ask him if he was a good sailor?"

"No, I didn't think of it."

"He'd probably have told you if he wasn't."

"I guess so—he wasn't slow at raising other objections. Of course, he might prefer to sleep the trip away —that's a thought. Can you do anything about sleeping tablets?"

"I believe I've got a few at the flat," Corinne said. "I don't use them often."

"Why should you? Clear conscience, and all that. No unsatisfied urges."

Corinne wrinkled her nose at him. "How about about clothes for Banda? And toilet things? He won't be bringing anything with him, will he?"

"No, just himself. I'll get him a toilet kit for the first morning in France, so he doesn't look too scruffy when he leaves us. He can buy his own clothes when he's over there. He'll know what he wants, and we'll have quite enough stuff to take as it is."

Corinne nodded. "When are we going to do our packing?"

"Well, you can go up to your flat and do yours whenever you like. Nearer the time, of course. I'll shove my things in a case when I take the wine racks."

"How much luggage are we going to allow ourselves?"

"One suitcase each, I'd say. But we can pack as many other cases as we like, and have them sent on afterward. That reminds me, I must drop a line to Dobson and put him in the picture—ask him to handle our affairs after we've gone. I'll write to him just before we leave." Bliss made another note. "Now, how about your car? Do you want to ship it, or will you sell it and get another when you're over there?"

"I think I'll sell it," Corinne said. "I'd like a change. I shall buy a smart little sports car that does a hundred miles an hour."

Bliss grinned. "I knew you were a fast type. Well, you won't be able to sell it until the last minute. We'll be needing it right up to the end. Still, that's no problem—you can easily fix something with your garage. Then, of course, we'll want another car—an expendable one. But that won't be till we're almost ready. Anything else for the list?"

"Maps of France for both of us," Corinne said. "And we mustn't forget to arrange where we're going to meet."

"We're not likely to do that. We'll choose a spot when we've got the maps."

Humming softly to himself—"Hold the Fort for I Am

Coming"—Bliss considered his list. "That's quite a good start, anyway. We can add to it as we get new ideas."

"I've got a new idea," Corinne said.

"What's that?"

She held out her glass. "Another Martini, please."

Bliss had a little trouble in finding a shop that sold the sort of wine racks he wanted, but he finally tracked down some suitable ones at a large wine merchant's in Brighton. They were made of a light plastic material, were easy to carry, and had a capacity of two dozen bottles each. Bliss bought three racks—two for the notional Romanée Conti and a third to hold some odd bottles that he'd accumulated at the flat. Three racks would look more like a cellar, he thought, if anyone happened to notice them. He paid cash, had them wrapped up together in a large sheet of wrapping paper, and carried them out to the Mercedes, where they went comfortably into the boot. From the wine merchant's he went on to Woolworth's to attend to the second item on his list—the fastening for the inside of the chest. He settled for the simplest thing he could find—a metal hook and eye, with appropriate screws.

That evening he drove alone to Hampstead.

He approached the flat with unusual circumspection. The possibility that any of Olsen's friends might be hanging about there, hoping for his return, seemed extremely remote, but there was just a chance that one of Kirby's plain-clothes men might be keeping an eye on the place. And it wouldn't do for the police to see him creeping back on his own, after all the fuss he'd made about the danger—especially with a very large parcel over his shoulder, which would certainly attract attention. If there was anyone waiting around within sight of the front door, it might be better to use the fire escape and force the window catch. Anyway, a quick look first . . . Bliss parked the Mercedes a hundred yards from the house and walked smartly around the block. There were the usual lines of cars on both sides of the road, but they all appeared to be unoccupied. He passed three pedestrians, an elderly woman and two boys, and that was all. A bold approach seemed justified. He returned to the Mercedes and drove to number 15. For a moment he sat quietly outside in the car, looking into the house. There was no visible movement in the lighted hall or through the upper-landing windows—only, through gaps in curtains, the greenish glare of television sets. At peak viewing times there was rarely much coming or going on the stairs. Bliss collected the wine racks from the boot, walked quickly into the house, climbed to his flat and let himself in. Good! He'd made it. No one had seen him. And with luck, no one would ever know he'd been there.

Treading softly, he felt his way around in the darkness, drawing heavy curtains over all the windows before he switched on a light. Then he carried the wine racks into the study and got straight down to work.

He tried at first just standing the racks against the wall in the glory hole, but the floor was uneven and he saw that he'd have to fasten them if they were to stay upright. It was a simple carpentering job for a handyman, and Bliss had always fancied himself as a handyman. He cleared a space, got out his tools, gouged three holes in the plaster with the minimum of noise, plugged them, and screwed the racks to the wall. Then he carried seven assorted bottles of wine from his sitting room bar and disposed them around one of the racks. So far, so good.

Now for the chest. Bliss drew it carefully out into the study, where there was more room to work, and considered the problem of the fastening. Since the lid would theoretically be locked when the chest was taken away, the hook and eye must be a tight enough fit to leave no play. A bit tricky to arrange that, operating from the outside. It would be a case of trial and error. . . . For fifteen minutes he worked with bradawl and screwdriver, fixing the eye to the inside of the lid and the hook to the inside of the front of the chest, next to the lock. When he'd finished he checked the distances. They seemed about right for a good fit, but there was only one way to make sure. He took a torch from a drawer of his desk, squeezed his bulk into the chest, and lowered the lid. Cramped and contorted, he switched on the torch and pressed the hook into the eye. It went home with a click. Fine! No play at all. He pulled at the hook to get it out again. It didn't move. He pulled harder, but he couldn't budge it. The damned thing was too tight. It was jammed.

He lay still for a moment, sweat pouring off him. Take it quietly, fellow, he told himself. Keep calm. Think what to do. . . . He looked up at the hook. . . . Yes—that might do it. . . . He gripped the torch firmly and jabbed at the point of the hook, trying to push it back through the eye. The point dented the base of the torch, but that was all. No good . . . What about the other end of the hook, where it was fastened by screws to the oak? Perhaps he could loosen it a

little, move it nearer to the eye. For several seconds
he banged away, without visible effect. He could get
no power behind the blows. There was only room for
short-arm jabs. To add to his troubles, the torch suddenly packed up. He continued to jab in the near-dark-
ness, his only light the narrow rays that came through
the crack in the lid. A fraction of an inch would do
it. A hair's breadth of give in the screws. He battered
away till his cramped muscles could bear the pain no
longer. He tried once more to pull the hook out. It
was as tight as ever.

At that moment Bliss was as close to panic as he'd
ever been in his life. This could be nemesis! If he
couldn't get out of the chest by his own efforts, it
wasn't just the enterprise that was finished. The
chances were that he'd be finished too. No one would
come to the flat. No one in the house would hear his
muffled shouts through the thick chest walls and the
solid, carpeted floor. No one knew he was there except
Corinne, and it would never occur to her that he could
have got into such trouble. It might be days before she
got around to doing anything. By that time, he'd be
dead. And what a death!

He took a grip on himself. If he panicked, he'd be
lost. Somehow, he'd got to find a way out. There *must*
be a way. Maybe if he turned over onto his stomach
he could force the lid open by heaving up with his
bottom. But once on his front, he might find himself as
helpless as a tortoise on its back. A last resort, that.
He lay still, conserving his strength, thinking about
the hook and eye, picturing them. What he needed was
something that would prize open the end of the hook
—something that would give him a bit of leverage. A

coin . . . ? No, too small. A key . . . ? Perhaps he
could wedge a key in the open end of the hook—that
would give him leverage. Or better still . . . Hope returned as an idea suddenly came to him. He groped
for his bunch of keys. Panting and sweating, he eased
them from his pocket. One of them was a steel key.
He'd inherited it with the old-fashioned mortise lock
on the flat door, which he now rarely used. It had a
hollow shaft. He reached up, found the point of the
hook with his thumb, and pushed the hollow end of the
key over the point. Then he started to lever the point
outward. For a moment he believed it was moving.
Then the end of the key snapped.

Had the point moved? He pulled again on the hook.
It shot out of the eye quite easily.

He raised the lid and heaved himself out. No Mistle-
toe Bough for him, after all. But, by golly, it had been
a near thing! He must have been crazy to shut himself
in on his own. *Too* bloody confident, for once! He
mopped his face and flexed his aching muscles. Presently he went to the bar and poured himself a stiff
shot of whiskey and drank it neat. He felt better after
that. Not to worry—a miss was as good as a mile. And
what a story he'd have to tell Corinne! Now, back to
work. He replaced the chest in the glory hole and
started on his other chores. Suitcases out. Books in one
of them—any old books. A few carefully chosen clothes
in another, with various papers and documents that he
didn't want to leave behind. More clothes in a third,
to be sent on afterward. He felt quite cheerful again
now. As he worked he hummed softly to himself—
"Ye Suffering Saints Fresh Courage Take." . . .

By ten o'clock his packing was finished. Just a couple more jobs from his list, and then he could go. He unlatched the sash window in the study, so that it would be ready for Banda when he came. He also emptied the black deed box of its incriminating contents, destroying the paper and stuffing the assortment of keys and rubber stamps into his pockets. Then he put out all the lights, opened up the curtains, walked quickly down to the street, and drove off. On his way back to Sussex he stopped for a moment by a roadside pond and disposed of the rubber stamps and the keys.

"As a matter of interest," Bliss said, "what *would* you have done if I hadn't shown up?"

It was nine o'clock next morning. Bliss and Corinne were lingering over their breakfast coffee. Bliss, still a little stiff in his joints but otherwise in good shape after a fair night's sleep, had just come to the end of his horrifying story. Corinne was looking suitably solemn.

"I've no idea," she said. "Does it matter now?"

"It does, in a way. I'm curious to know how you'd handle a crisis."

"Testing my nerve, are you?"

"Call it an exercise."

"Well . . ." There was a pause while Corinne considered. "I'd certainly have been getting very worried by now if I hadn't heard from you. I'd have telephoned the flat, of course, and got no answer. I'd probably have waited to see if you telephoned me—I don't know how long. Sometime during the day, I'd probably have decided that you'd run into trouble with Olsen's friends."

"Really?"

"It would have been the obvious thing, wouldn't it?"

"From your point of view, I suppose it would. And what would you have done?"

"Well," Corinne said, "there'd have been two possibilities, wouldn't there? I could have rung Kirby and told him you'd had to go to the flat for something, and hadn't come back. Or I could have gone up to the flat myself to see if I could find out anything."

"The choice would have made quite a difference. Which would it have been?"

Corinne met Bliss's quizzical gaze with a cool smile. "Guess!" she said.

When Bliss called at the reception office after breakfast he found that the first batch of letters had arrived from the flat. They were in a large envelope addressed to Henry Freeman, with no indication that they'd come from the Yard. Only one of the letters was of any consequence, but that one was very important indeed. It was a confirmation from the Crédit Lyonnais in Aix-en-Provence that the sum of £25,000 had been credited to Bliss's account. He passed it to Corinne without comment.

A sparkle came into her eyes as she read it. "That's wonderful!" She had never quite been able to believe that the promised deposit would turn into actual cash at a bank.

"Not a bad lump of lolly, is it? Whatever happens now, our little venture will have paid off."

"I'll say!" Corinne handed the letter back. "You'd better destroy this, hadn't you?"

Bliss nodded. "Item one on the day's agenda."

"I wonder you dare let the police handle post like that."

"Why not? They wouldn't open it. I think it's a rather good ploy. The more I seem to trust them, the more they'll trust me. Shows I'm an upright citizen with nothing to hide."

Corinne smiled. "You're incorrigible."

"As a matter of fact," Bliss said, "it's a situation we might exploit a bit further."

"How?"

"Well, I've been thinking. This idea that we're scared stiff of the gang will be wearing a bit thin by the time the trial's over, if nothing at all happens. I reckon it needs a bit of a booster."

"Not with me, it doesn't."

"Perhaps not, but it may with Kirby. The one thing we can't afford is for him to have any last-minute doubts about why we want to get out of the country so fast and so secretly. An anonymous threatening letter to myself could do a lot of good."

"You mean *you'd* write it?"

"Sure."

Corinne gave a slightly dubious nod. "You don't think it would be gilding the lily?"

"No—just reviving it."

"M'm. Well, I suppose it would be all right—as long as Kirby believed it was genuine."

"He'd have no reason not to. Especially if the first person to notice the letter was the sleuth who collects my mail. That's what I meant about exploiting the postal arrangements. It would be most convincing."

"*Would* the sleuth notice it?"

"He would if it was addressed in large, flamboyant writing. Look, let's go and buy a few things and try it out."

They got to work on the letter that afternoon in the privacy of Corinne's room. Bliss had laid out their purchases on a table—a pair of surgical gloves; a large white envelope of a common variety, in a paper bag; and a felt-tipped, self-inking pen, a product of Japan. The message was to be written on a piece of rough brown paper that had been used to wrap up some parcel of Corinne's.

Bliss put on the gloves and flattened out the brown paper. "Right—now what shall we say? Something like 'If you shop Olsen you're a dead man'?"

Corinne considered. "Would they use the word 'shop'? Writing to you, I mean?"

"M'm—perhaps not. Come to that, I suppose I've already shopped him. From their point of view, the damage is done. Something simpler, eh? How about 'You'll get yours'? A crude threat, straight to the point."

"Horribly to the point," Corinne said.

"I don't like the 'you'll,' though—it doesn't sound right. I know! 'You got yours coming.' Nice and vulgar. How's that?"

"Not bad at all."

"Let's settle for that, then." Bliss took the pen and scrawled the words, thick and black, in big capital letters on the brown paper. Then he addressed the envelope, in only slightly smaller capitals, to "Mr. M. Bliss, 15 Bampton Gardens, London." He sat back, surveying his handiwork. "There—what do you think of it?"

"It's certainly most convincing," Corinne said. "But won't the police expect to find fingerprints on the paper and envelope?"

Bliss shook his head. "On the contrary, they'll expect not to. They'll know any competent crook would wear gloves. Now where are we going to post it? It ought to be somewhere in London."

"If you like, I'll post it," Corinne said. "I was thinking of driving up tomorrow anyway. I want to arrange about selling my car. I'll drop it in somewhere in the West End."

"Okay—fine." Bliss slipped the letter into the paper bag the envelope had been in, and drew off his gloves. "Better lock it up in your case for the time being. And remember to handle it by the edges when you take it out of the bag. Right—now let's drive around and get rid of the pen and the gloves."

The next day was a busy one for both of them.

Bliss was able to tick off several more items on his list during a morning of shopping in Eastbourne. He bought the labels for the chest; the outsize box of matches; a water bottle, some Marzine tablets, a toilet kit and a slab of chocolate for Banda, and two road maps of northern France. The item "bale of straw" was still outstanding, but on the way back to the Blue Boar he was able to clear that up, too. As he drove along a byroad below the Downs, he noticed the remains of an old stack in a field. He stopped beside the gate and took a leisurely look around. There was no one in the field, no car in sight on the road. He nipped over the gate, helped himself to a rectangular bale of pressed straw, and quickly locked it away in the boot.

He felt rather pleased with his morning's work. Several more pieces of the jigsaw plan had been neatly slotted into place.

Corinne had an equally fruitful day. She posted the anonymous letter in the Strand, drove on to Knightsbridge, and packed her clothes and belongings into three large suitcases and a trunk. She moved the little Queen Anne table, and the suitcase she proposed to take with her, into the hall, ready for the police to pick up when they called with the van on D-night. Then she drove around to the garage which had regularly serviced her Mini. She would like to sell the car, she said, as she was going abroad, but she'd need it until the very night she went. Would they collect it if she left it outside her house? She'd send them the key by letter. They said they'd be happy to do that, and a price was agreed. It wasn't, Corinne felt, a very good price, but with the prospect of wealth coming rapidly nearer, she didn't bother to argue.

Now they were watching the post again. Two mornings passed without anything arriving for Henry Freeman. Then, on the third day, the anonymous letter found its way back, in an even larger envelope than usual. Bliss immediately phoned Kirby at the Yard and told him about it, in a voice sharp with anxiety. There was a little pause at the other end. Then Kirby said he'd drive down at once and have a look at it.

He arrived just before noon, in a gray Jaguar without police markings. Bliss and Corinne joined him in the parked car, where they could talk privately. "Here's the letter," Bliss said, handing it over. He sat in strained silence, watching Kirby's face, waiting for the first comment. He could see the inspector was much put out by the incident. Probably worrying again about his witness's morale . . .

"Well, I'm sorry about this." Kirby pushed the brown paper back into its envelope. "Very trying for you both."

"That's putting it mildly," Bliss said. "We're still in a state of shock. Do you think there's any chance of finding out who sent it?"

Kirby shook his head. "I doubt it. I'll give it to the lab, of course, but the paper and envelope could have come from anywhere, and there aren't likely to be any useful prints."

Bliss nodded gravely. "What I don't understand, Inspector, is why they bothered to warn me. I can understand they want to get me—it's what I've been afraid of all along. But why send a letter? Why not just act?"

"That's exactly the point I was coming to," Kirby said. "The answer, I'm sure, is that they've no intention of acting. They must realize you're under police protection, and that means they're powerless. So what's left to them? All they can do is get a bit of bile out of their system by sending you a threatening letter. They're just trying to upset you."

"They've certainly done that," Corinne said. "It was a horrible thing to read."

"I know, Miss Lake, but I do assure you again that there's no need to worry. These men don't know where you are, and they won't find out. We shall take every precaution when Mr. Bliss is in town for the trial, and on the night you leave. You can safely put the whole thing out of your mind."

"Well, we'll try, of course," Bliss said. "I suppose your explanation could be the right one."

"I'm sure it is."

"Still, I must say that the letter makes getting away seem even more attractive. How are the arrangements going, Inspector?"

Kirby brightened. "Very well indeed, sir. In fact, they're almost finished. We've got the Bedford van for you and we've checked it over. It cost about three hundred pounds—I'll be letting you have a note of the exact amount. I've also been in touch with the Bank of England and they're agreeable to the capital transfer you mentioned. All you need do is instruct your own bank when you're ready. We've done the paper work in connection with the export of your car and of the van, so you'll have no trouble there. And the carriers have agreed to cooperate in the matter of travel date."

"Splendid," Bliss said. "Are you any nearer knowing when that date is likely to be?"

"Yes, I was going to ring you about that. The hearing has been set down for next Monday, and we should get the verdict within the week." Kirby smiled at Corinne. "So your anxieties, Miss Lake, are almost over."

Corinne gave a little sigh. "How marvelous it will be!"

Bliss watched Corinne closely during the period before the trial, fearing she might get jumpy as the time for action approached. But far from showing any sign of nerves, she seemed to grow more practical and purposeful with every day that passed. She took a keen interest in the choice of their French rendezvous, spreading a map out in her room and discussing the alternatives with all the enthusiasm of an ardent route finder. She had managed, too, to get hold of a Bedford instruction book at a secondhand shop in Brighton, and she spent a whole afternoon familiarizing herself with the instrument panel and the gears. In some ways, Bliss reflected, she had a surprisingly masculine mind.

Bliss himself, though eager for the starting gun, was completely at ease. Only a stroke of really bad luck, he felt, could spoil the enterprise now. All the preparations had gone smoothly. Kirby was wholly on their side. Not a breath of suspicion had been roused. The plans for D-night had been thoroughly discussed, and were now perfected. The trial would be a bit of a bore, of course, but it held no dangers and raised no problems. Olsen's fate might be a matter of vital importance to Kirby, but the outcome of the trial was of no consequence to the conspirators—unless, as Bliss suggested to Corinne in a teasing moment, the jury disagreed! Short of that, their plan would go into action whatever the verdict. When Kirby telephoned once more during the week end about the trial arrangements, Bliss was able to assure him that, apart from a slight residual anxiety about his own safety, he was in a tranquil and confident frame of mind.

Kirby's precautions on the day of the trial left nothing to chance.

At eight o'clock that morning, Corinne drove Bliss into Brighton. There he was met by a burly plain-clothes man, who accompanied him to Victoria on a fast train. Two more plain-clothes men were waiting for him at the barrier. They escorted him to a car, whisked him to the Old Bailey, smuggled him in by a back door, and continued to keep watch over him in a private room.

Bliss was called to give his evidence soon after the prosecution's opening statement. Whatever had gone before, or might come later, there was singularly little drama in the court while he was there. Panoply, yes, and a heavy dignity, but little feeling of tension. Jack Olsen sat hunched and gloomy in the dock, looking as though he'd already resigned himself to an adverse verdict. If any of his muscle men were present, they were up in the crowded public gallery, out of sight.

Bliss's examination-in-chief followed lines almost identical with those in the lower court. The cross-examination was a good deal more probing and persistent, but at no time dangerous. Any faint qualms Bliss might have felt about the possibility of his own past activities coming to light were soon dispelled. Obviously the defense hadn't been able to find out anything useful about him and counsel made no attempt to cast doubt on his good faith. What he did do was ask much more detailed questions about those few vital seconds in the mews, plugging away at problems of distance, lighting and shadows, and the difficulties of making any reliable identification in such circumstances. But he got nowhere. Bliss, playing impeccably his role of disinterested and conscientious citizen, held his ground quietly but firmly, and conceded nothing. By the end of the day he had done his job.

As he left the courtroom, the police guard closed around him again. A red Mini took him to the Yard and a plain-clothes man drove him down to Sussex in another car. By dinner time he was safely back at the Blue Boar as Henry Freeman.

With Corinne, he followed the next day's proceedings on the radio and from very full reports in the evening newspapers. There had been some interesting developments. Kirby had given evidence of the statement he'd taken from Olsen, the alibi statement, and had told of the discovery he'd made at the house on the river. Cross-examination had indicated that the defense were standing by their alibi. Their line had been that the bird's nest with its eggs might well have remained in the hollow end of the bar on a first or second raising, and fallen out on a third. Who could say with certainty? There had been some ornithological discussion, and in the afternoon the jury had visited the site to see the bar in operation and draw their own conclusions.

That evening, Kirby called Bliss on the telephone. He sounded very cheerful. The timetable of the trial was now pretty clear, he said. A verdict could be expected on the Thursday, the fourth day, and he was going ahead with firm bookings for Corinne and Bliss on that basis. He ran over the final arrangements for the evening, confirmed that everything was in order, and said he hoped to be at the flat himself around half-past eleven to see Bliss on his way.

Of the few items still left unticked on Bliss's list, the main one was the acquisition of an expendable car. A bit dodgy, this, as he'd always realized, if it was to be done without leaving a trail. But he had his plan. Early on the Wednesday morning he drove with Corinne to the Brixton area of south London. The main road there, as he'd noted on his journeys to and from the flat, was lined with enormous sales lots displaying hundreds of cheaply priced secondhand cars. Bliss parked the Mini in a side street, pulled a newly purchased cloth cap well down over his forehead, donned a pair of dark glasses, drew on a pair of washleather gloves, and set off on foot to pick his bargain. He chose a site where the salesman looked particularly unprepossessing, stated his requirements in a strong Cockney accent, and in ten minutes had paid £62 in cash for a Morris Minor of inconspicuous color that was not quite on its last legs. No questions had been asked, and no information given. So far, so very good . . .

On the way back to Sussex, in convoy with Corinne in the Mini, Bliss stopped three times. Once at a hardware store, where he bought a two-gallon plastic container. Once at a garage, where he had the container filled with petrol and stowed it in the Morris's boot. Once beside a wood, where the ground looked soft. Choosing his moment he walked in among the trees, scooped out a shallow hole among some roots, and buried his new cloth cap.

That evening, he and Corinne proceeded separately to the vicinity of Lushington, Bliss in the Morris and Corinne in the Mini. At a quiet spot Bliss, still wearing his washleather gloves, raised the bonnet of the Morris and scored out the engine and chassis number with a hammer and a sharp-edged punch he'd found among the tools. He also loosened the screws holding the two number plates. Then, as dusk fell, he drove to the hill above Max Banda's house. He parked the Morris on the grass verge just above the chalk quarry, lightly jacked up one of the wheels to give the impression of temporary trouble, locked the car, and walked away southward along the winding road. In a couple of minutes Corinne came by in the Mini and picked him up.

With rising excitement, now, they drove back to the hotel. In the privacy of the bathroom, Bliss got rid of the Morris's logbook.

The evening paper again had a long account of the day's proceedings at the trial, and it was clear that things were going badly for Olsen. Most of the sitting had been devoted to the examination and cross-examination of the three "friends" who'd said they'd been playing poker with him at the river house, and they'd been easy game for the prosecution. Though their stories had seemed to tally under the helpful guidance of the defense counsel, numerous contradictions had appeared once the prosecution had got down to details, and their evidence had ended in confusion. Bliss, judging their performance by his own exacting professional standards, declared himself shocked.

Kirby telephoned the verdict at three o'clock on the Thursday afternoon. "It's all over, Mr. Bliss." His tone was jubilant.

"Guilty, I take it?"

"Yes, guilty. The jury were only out for twenty minutes. Olsen's got seven years."

"Well, I congratulate you," Bliss said.

"We owe it to you, sir, more than to anybody. You did a fine job—better than you know. With luck, we've pretty well broken up that gang. We picked up Olsen's three buddies after the verdict and charged them with perjury, and one of them's admitted it, so they'll be inside, too, before long."

"Quite a day for the police," Bliss said.

"Yes, indeed—makes up for some of the disappointments. Well, Mr. Bliss, everything's set for tonight. We'll meet as arranged—eleven-thirty at your flat. And give my best wishes to Miss Lake. I probably shan't see her again."

"I will," Bliss said. "Okay, Inspector. 'Bye for now."

He hung up, and went off quickly to find Corinne. He was feeling pretty jubilant, too. The waiting was over, the stage was set. Now for the last act.

IV

BLISS ARRIVED at the hill just as dusk was beginning to fall. The time by his watch, which he'd synchronized with Corinne's, was exactly eight-twenty. He parked the Mercedes at its old spot on the verge of the winding road, its bonnet turned to the south for a quick getaway after the crash. Then, with a few minutes in hand, he climbed to the seat and took a look at Banda's house through the glasses. What he saw was reassuring. Lights were visible through the curtained windows of the bedroom and there was a green glow from the television set. All the downstairs lights were out. The old boy was carrying out his instructions. He was on the ball. Now he would be waiting for the big bang. All ready to slip through the culvert to the field. And that shouldn't give him any trouble. There'd been a little rain the day before, but not enough to make the stream rise.

Bliss turned the glasses on the guard cars. The two policemen were sitting in their respective cars. Neither of them seemed to be doing anything. Just waiting. Wishing, no doubt, it was time for their relief. They'd be glad of a bit of action!

On the twin roads, nothing moved. The usual eve-

ning quiet had settled over the landscape. The calm
before the storm . . .

Bliss returned to the Mercedes, slung the binoculars
on the back seat, put on his washleather gloves, and
walked quickly to the quarry. The Morris was just as
he'd left it. In the failing light he let the jacked-up
wheel down and detached the two loose number
plates. He glanced at his watch again. Eight forty-four.
A moment later he caught the sound of a car coming
up the winding road from the south. As it rounded the
last bend its lights flashed off and on. Corinne in the
Mini, right on time. She stopped beside him and he
pushed the number plates through the open rear window. "A *bientôt!*" he called softly. "See you in
France." She gave a little wave and drove on toward
the copse.

As the noise of the Mini died away, Bliss stood listening. No more cars were approaching. No footsteps
sounded on the road. He had the place to himself.
And darkness was falling fast. This was it. Zero hour
. . . He took the plastic container from the boot and
unlocked the car. He unscrewed the top of the container and splashed the two gallons of petrol over the
car, soaking the upholstery, the engine and the body
work. He flung the empty container on the floor inside
and shut the door.

From his pocket he took the jumbo box of matches.
He slid it open an inch or so and held it ready in his
right hand. With his left he released the car's hand
brake and turned the wheels toward the unfenced
edge of the quarry. He began to push. The turf was
smooth, the slope slightly downward. The car quickly
gathered momentum, reached the edge, checked for a

second as the front wheels went down and the chassis scraped the ground, then pitched over the side. As it disappeared, Bliss ignited the whole box of matches, tossed it after the car, and stepped back. There was a crash of breaking glass as the Morris plunged through the thorn bushes to the quarry floor. A moment later, a great blast of flame shot into the air.

Bliss retreated around the shoulder of the hill and waited tensely in the shadows. The success or failure of the whole plot could turn on what happened in the next few minutes. Not that he could do much about it now, if his judgment had been wrong, but he wanted to know. Sixty seconds passed. Anxious, interminable seconds. Then, above the roar of the fire, he heard voices. Two men, shouting to each other as they climbed to the quarry from below. The guards . . .

Bliss drew a long breath and turned away. The plan had worked, and with luck it would go on working. The heat of the fire would make any close approach to the wreck impossible for quite a time. Even when the flames were out it would take the police some while, in that tangle of thorn, to discover there had been no one in the car. And the significance of the fact wouldn't strike them at once. They'd probably think someone had shoved it over the edge to get rid of it, and then cleared off. People were always dumping unwanted cars, and the fire could have happened by accident. Petrol pouring from the tank—a spark—metal on flint . . . At some time, of course, they'd wonder. When the bedroom light was still on in the morning. When Banda didn't appear. When the cleaning woman arrived and couldn't get in. They'd know, then, that they'd been hoaxed. But by that time, Banda would be out of their reach. And the burned-out car would tell them nothing of the man who'd hoaxed them. It wouldn't even give them a useful fingerprint. Bliss had taken care of everything.

Satisfied, he returned quickly to the Mercedes, free-wheeled down the south side of the hill, and headed the car for London.

Bliss had been right about Banda being ready and waiting. From sunset onward, he had been standing expectantly behind the drawn curtains of his open bedroom window, listening for the crash above the chatter of his television, fearful he might miss his cue. For weeks, now, he had thought of little else but this moment of flight, building up its hazards to monstrous proportions in his mind. At the sudden din, his heart pounded as though it would burst. That was it!—the noise of breaking glass was unmistakable. His mouth went dry at the need for action. Should he go at once? Should he wait a bit? He opened the window a little wider. As the flames rose, and the reverberations of the crash died down, he heard a car door slam on the northern road. Then shouts, and the sound of running footsteps. Soon, lights flashed on the hillside. Torches —two of them. Both the guards were out there. The way must be clear. He turned up the television and hurried downstairs. In the sitting room he ripped the phone connection from the wall. Then he let himself out through the back door and made for the culvert.

Where Bliss had been wrong was in thinking the old boy would have an easy passage after he'd left. The sky was overcast, the night already very dark. Nothing on the ground was visible. Banda slipped as he descended the grassy bank and sat down heavily on his bottom. In the culvert he got both his feet wet. As he emerged from it he straightened up too precipitately and banged his head on the roof. Between the first and second fields he couldn't find the gate in the darkness and rushed wildly to and fro. Afterward, by the hedge, there was a lot of soft ground. . . . Forgery was easier!

Corinne had backed the Mini into the copse and was waiting with lights out for Banda's arrival. She was getting a bit concerned. Ten minutes had passed since the crash and the flash from the quarry, and he still hadn't come. Surely he wasn't going to muff his chance. . . .

She got out of the car and stood listening. She could hear the voices of the guards at the quarry. Nothing else. After the din, the silence around her was almost tangible. Then, from somewhere along the field hedge, she caught the crackle of a breaking twig. A bulky shape loomed for a moment against the sky above a gate. At last . . . ! She called "This way!" softly and went to meet the shape. Banda came stumbling toward her over the uneven grass of the verge. He was breathing heavily. She took his arm, guiding him. "Have you got everything? Passport, mustache, glasses?" He gave an affirmative grunt, slapping his breast pocket. She steered him to the car, bundled him into the passenger seat, climbed in beside him, and drove off on sidelights only.

"You were an awfully long time," she said. "What kept you?"

"It was rough in the field. I lost my way. I fell. I have mud on me." He brushed at his clothes with his hand. He was still fighting for breath. "Forgive me—I am not used to these excitements."

"That's all right." Corinne switched on the Mini's headlights and put on speed. "You can relax now, your troubles are over."

"I would like to think so." He sounded very agitated. Hardly the man, Corinne thought, that you'd choose to have with you in a tight spot. He might be clever, but he just didn't have any backbone. He'd crumple at the first crisis.

Banda turned nervously as a light shone through the rear window. "There is a car behind us."

Corinne nodded. "What about it?"

"Perhaps we are being followed."

"Of course we're not. How could we be? Stop worrying, Mr. Banda. I shall deliver you, all right." The pursuing lights swung away. "There you are, you see—it's turned off."

Banda heaved a sigh. "How long will it take us to get to London?"

"About ninety minutes, with luck."

"You know the way?"

"I ought to. I've driven over it often enough."

"Are your tires good?"

"Oh, *really!* Why don't you lie back and have a sleep?"

"Sleep! You are joking, Miss Lake. Not that I do not trust your driving. You drive very well."

"Yes," Corinne said. "I know."

"Are all the arrangements made? Is everything as planned?"

"Yes, everything's fine."

"I heard the result of the trial at six o'clock. Since then I have been on tenterhooks."

"I can imagine."

There was a little silence. Then Banda began to talk again. He seemed to have recovered his poise. "It was a brilliant plan," he said. "The car crash. So simple, so successful. I begin to think your fiancé is a man of genius."

Corinne smiled in the darkness of the car. "I'm sure he'd be the first to agree with you. Actually, he's not my fiancé."

"No?"

"No—we're just good friends. Working together on the job."

"I see . . . So you will not be marrying him?"

"I shouldn't think so for a moment. The suggestion hasn't been made."

"Then what are your plans, Miss Lake, if I may ask?"

"I haven't got any definite plans," Corinne said. "To see a bit more of the world, I suppose. To enjoy myself. To have a lovely life in the sun."

"A lovely life in the sun—yes, that is an attractive prospect. It requires money, of course, a great deal of money. More, perhaps, than you will have. Capital melts away so quickly in the sun. . . . However, I wish you all success. And happiness."

"Thank you . . . What are you going to do, Mr. Banda?"

"I? Well—assuming that everything happens as Mr. Bliss has promised—I think I shall go first to Menton. You know it?"

"Only by name."

"It is a small town on the Mediterranean frontier between France and Italy. By far the pleasantest place, in my opinion, on the whole of the Riviera. And certainly with the best climate. It is sheltered by high mountains, and the mistral rarely blows. . . . Yes, I shall go there for a while, to rest and recover from my ordeal. I have—I think—a delightful villa at Menton. On Cap Martin. Between Menton and Monte Carlo."

"You think . . . ? Don't you know?"

"I have never seen it. I was negotiating for its purchase—through an intermediary and in a different name, not my own—when my empire, as the newspapers called it, collapsed. It was to be my refuge, my hideaway in case of trouble. There, as George Wilson, I would be able to retreat from the eyes of the world for a while. I, too, had plans for changing my appearance. I had perfected all my arrangements. Unfortunately, on the very day the purchase was completed, I was arrested."

"Too bad!"

"It seemed so, but now, thanks to you and Mr. Bliss, I look forward to enjoying it—at least for a few weeks, until I feel strong enough to move on. . . . The Villa Hirondelle, it is called. It stands, I am told, high on the cliffside, overlooking a sapphire-blue sea, in a garden of lemons and oranges and vines. Below, there is a private beach of white sand, with a little swimming pool built into the rocks. And only a few minutes away by car are all the pleasures and excitements of Monte Carlo."

"It sounds idyllic."

Banda sighed. "It will need only a beautiful woman to make it perfect."

"I'm sure you'll find one," Corinne said.

"Perhaps . . . Since meeting you, Miss Lake, my standards have risen, my taste has become more exacting. It will be less easy for me, now, to find someone with whom I can share my life and my wealth. . . . Of course, if by some fortunate chance you should happen to be in Menton yourself . . ."

"I don't think it's very likely," Corinne said. "Still, you never know." Her mind, at that moment, was on other things. She had slowed down and was gazing ahead with great concentration. Presently she pulled up.

Banda looked out. All he could see was a pond by the roadside. "Why have we stopped? Is something wrong?"

"Nothing at all. I won't be a minute." Corinne got out, glanced up and down the road, took the Morris's number plates from the back of the car, and flung them out into the pond to join Bliss's rubber stamps and keys. "Our dustbin," she said with a smile as she slid back in behind the wheel.

It was just after ten-thirty when they reached Bampton Gardens.

"I'll drive you around the block and show you where to go," Corinne said. She had promised Bliss to make one reconnaissance circuit before she dropped Banda off, and since she was in the Mini, not the Mercedes, and hadn't got to stop at the flat, it didn't seem too dangerous a concession. In fact, as she drove around the quiet suburban roads she had to admit to herself that her fear of the gang had probably been quite unnecessary. The man sitting in a car immediately opposite number 15 was almost certainly Inspector Kirby's promised watchdog. And no one else was taking any interest in the house. Cranford Gardens, the parallel road at the rear, was deserted; its parked cars were all unoccupied. As the Mini cruised past, Corinne pointed out the green garden gate that Banda had to go through. "It's always left unlocked," she said, "and the bottom of the fire escape is right opposite the gate. You can't miss it."

She pulled up on the corner. "So this is where I leave you. Oh, one more thing." She felt in her bag. "Here —sleeping tablets. Mike said I was to give them to you."

"Thank you." Banda put them in his pocket. "But I don't know that I shall use them."

"I should, if I were you. You'll only lie and worry if you don't. Still, it's up to you. As long as you don't give me any trouble on the road."

"I shall try not to do that."

"Good."

Banda seemed reluctant to go. "What exactly will our schedule be?"

"About an hour and a half to Dover," Corinne told him. "Then you can reckon another two hours or so in the car bay of the ferry, and about half an hour to the rendezvous. I shan't stop to let you out till we join Mike."

"I understand." Banda opened the car door. "Well —now I suppose I must take my chance." He was very tense again. "Let us hope that no one sees me."

"I'm sure no one will. You'll be up there in a few seconds. Good luck, Mr. Banda. See you in France."

Banda forced a smile, got out of the car, and walked slowly away with the air of a man going to his execution.

The gate was on a latch. Banda raised it and went cautiously through. He could see what looked like a gravel path ahead of him. There were no lighted windows immediately around, but there was a general glow from distant street lamps that gave him all the light that he needed. He walked nervously up the gravel path, his footsteps crunching on the stones. The spiral of the fire escape loomed up in front of him. He began to climb, clinging to the handrail, not liking the height, not liking the way the structure creaked and moved under his feet. Not liking any part of it . . . But somehow he reached the top, and no one had called out to him, no one had asked him what he was doing. Bliss had been right once more. Suddenly a dog barked, quite close, and Banda almost fell. Sweat broke out all over him. He reached for the window with clammy hands, got his fingers under it, and pushed it up. The dog barked again. Someone shouted at it. Banda climbed in, and closed the window behind him, and groped in the darkness for something to sit down on. Anything. He was breathing hard. He hadn't even started his journey yet, and he felt exhausted.

Bliss reached Hampstead at ten forty-five, having traveled a somewhat longer route than the others. He, too, drove once around the block, alert for any sign of trouble. But all seemed well. The green gate, he noticed, was slightly ajar, which suggested that Corinne and Banda had done their stuff. He completed the circuit and parked just ahead of the guard car at the front of the house. The driver, he saw, was the man who'd taken him to the Blue Boar after the committal proceedings. Bliss walked back to speak to him. "Evening, officer."

"Evening, Mr. Bliss." The man glanced at his watch. "Cutting it a bit fine, aren't you, sir? You'll have to get a move on with your packing."

Bliss nodded. "I had a bit of trouble with the car." He glanced up and down the road. "No sign of the enemy?"

"Quiet as the grave, sir. Can I give you a hand at all?"

"I don't think so, thanks—I've not much to take up." Bliss returned to the Mercedes, collected the bale of straw from the boot, wrapped it in a rug to prevent the bits falling about, and carried it into the house. In the hall he passed a neighbor coming out and nodded affably. Then he climbed to the top floor and let himself in.

"You there, Banda?" he called softly.

There was no reply.

He walked through into the study. "Banda . . . ?"

A familiar voice said, "Yes, I am here."

"For God's sake, you don't have to act deaf with me." Bliss drew the curtains and switched on the light. Banda was sitting hunched in a chair. His face had a greenish tinge. "Did your trip go all right?"

"Yes, thank you."

"Any trouble getting into the house?"

"No."

"What are you looking so nervous about? Is something wrong?"

"Nothing in particular."

"Then relax, man! You haven't a thing to worry about. The whole operation's going like clockwork. All the arrangements are made and the police are rooting for us. What more do you want? Got your passport? All your things?"

"Yes."

"Right, we'd better get to work—we haven't much time." Bliss dragged the oak chest out of the glory hole and opened the lid. "There's the slit you'll breathe through," he said, pointing. "And that's the fastening you'll fix once you're inside. You'll have to do it by touch, but you'll find it's not difficult."

Banda examined the chest and the fastening. He looked like a man about to be thrown from an airplane without a parachute. Bliss was already busy with other things. He had taken the labels from his pocket and was selecting places for them. Three should be enough —he mustn't overdo it. He chose three different ones and stuck them on the lid of the chest and the two ends. The end ones read respectively "Fragile" and "Glass With Care." The one on the lid read "This Side Up."

Bliss stood back. "Yes, I think that'll do." He grinned at Banda. "At least you won't have to do the journey standing on your head!"

He fetched the bale of straw from the hall, broke the binding that held it together, and opened it up. Something live darted out and disappeared under the desk. "Only a mouse," Bliss said. Banda shuddered.

Bliss spread a thick layer of loose straw over the bottom of the chest. "Okay," he said. "Like to try it for size?"

Banda climbed in and lowered himself awkwardly onto the straw. He was about five inches shorter than the chest and several inches narrower. "Just the job," Bliss said. He fetched a pillow from the bedroom and put it under Banda's neck and shoulders. "How's that? Comfortable?"

"I have been more comfortable," Banda said.

"You will be again if you keep your head. For to-night you'll just have to grin and bear it." Bliss went to the bathroom and filled the water bottle. "Here's your liquid refreshment—but go easy on it! Now—what else? Slab of chocolate. Marzine tablets, in case you need them—but there's not much wind, you should have a good crossing. Got your sleeping pills?"

"Yes."

"Okay . . . Now I'm going to pack you in. You'll find it pretty warm, but it can't be helped."

Quickly and efficiently, Bliss put in the rest of the straw, padding it carefully on both sides of Banda's body and round his head and adding a thinner layer on top.

"Well, I guess that's it," he said. He looked at his watch. "I'm going to close up, now. The police will be here in about ten minutes and they'll carry you down. Don't make a sound while they're around, or we'll all have had it. Keep quiet, and you'll wake up in the morning a free man. Good luck!"

He lowered the lid. There was a little scratching inside as Banda fumbled with the fastening. Then the hook clicked into the eye. Bliss peered through the slit in the lid. He could see straw, but nothing else. "Okay?" he called.

"Yes," came a muffled voice. Then silence fell.

Bliss looked around, checking over the room. There were bits of straw all over the carpet, but that was as it should be. Nothing suspicious anywhere—nothing of interest to old Hawkeye. And everything ready for the movers. Suitcase of clothes. Two suitcases of books. And the chest. Bliss went to the bar and got himself a shot of whiskey. The next half hour was going to be very dicey. Probably the most dangerous part of the whole enterprise. He had complete faith in his plan, in Corinne, and in himself, but not much in Banda. It would be a miracle if the fellow didn't sneeze or cough or snore. No control, no nerve, no guts . . . He didn't deserve to be free!

Sounds reached Bliss from the street below. He went to the sitting-room window and looked down. Two men were getting out of a gray van. The Bedford. A car pulled up on the other side of the street and another man got out. Kirby. He was having a word with the driver of the guard car. Bliss went back to the study and tapped lightly on the chest. "They're here," he said, through the crack. "Remember—not a sound!" The bell rang in the hall and he went to the door. Kirby was there alone.

"Hullo, Inspector. Come on in."

"Evening, Mr. Bliss." Kirby stepped inside. "We'll leave the door open, shall we? My chaps are just coming up. Everything ready?"

"Yes—I've just finished."

"I gather you were delayed on the road."

Bliss nodded. "The damned petrol pump started playing up. I had to stop and fix it. It's always the way when you're in a hurry."

"I thought I could smell petrol," Kirby said.

"Yes, it shot all over me. Beastly stuff."

Footsteps sounded on the stairs and the two movers appeared. One of them was the tall sergeant who had accompanied Kirby on his first visit to the flat. "You remember Sergeant Groves," Kirby said. "And this is Sergeant Crewe."

Bliss nodded to them. "Everything's ready for you, gentlemen." He led the way to the study. "It's all rather heavy stuff, I'm afraid. Those two cases have got books in them, and the chest weighs a ton."

"We'll manage, sir," Groves said. "Let's take the chest first, George."

"You'll be as careful as you can with it, won't you? I don't want that wine shaken up more than you can help."

"We'll handle it like a baby," Groves said. He took one end, and Sergeant Crewe took the other, and they heaved it up. Bliss lit a cigarette and stood back, watching. He could feel his heart hammering. He was human, too! Neither of the men showed any surprise at the weight. Without much difficulty they maneuvered the chest out of the door. There was a slight bump as they turned the corner into the hall, and Bliss winced inwardly. Then they were off down the stairs.

Kirby took an envelope from his pocket. "Well, now, here are all your documents, Mr. Bliss. Passenger ticket, car ticket, French money, customs papers . . . I think you'll find everything's in order."

"I'm sure I will," Bliss said, but he checked through the contents all the same. "Yes—excellent."

"Sergeant Groves has got Miss Lake's tickets. He'll give them to her when he loads at Knightsbridge."

"Fine." Bliss ran the back of his hand across his forehead to prevent the sweat dripping into his eyes.

"Got a bit hot packing, eh?"

"Yes—I had to do it in such a rush." Bliss was listening for the return of the bearers, wondering why they were such a hell of a time. Surely the chest must be in the van by now. What were they waiting for? Then he relaxed as voices sounded on the stairs again. Quiet voices. Not the tone of men who'd found a body in a box.

Sergeant Groves came in smiling. "I don't think we broke any of your bottles, Mr. Bliss." He gathered up two of the cases and the other man picked up the third. Groves looked around. "That's the lot, is it?"

"That's the lot," Bliss said. "And thank you very much."

"It's been a pleasure." Groves turned to Kirby. "We'll be off, then, sir."

"All right, Sergeant. Take it easy."

"You'll make quite sure you're not tailed to Knightsbridge, won't you?" Bliss said, forcing a final note of apprehension into his voice. He was getting pretty bored with his line by now.

Groves nodded. "Leave it to us, sir—we're old hands." He followed the other man out. In a few moments Bliss heard the van door slam shut. An engine started up, and the van moved off.

Bliss looked down at the straw-covered floor. "Bit of a mess, isn't it? Never mind, I'll ask old Dobson to get someone to clear it up." He looked at his watch. "Well, I guess I should be on my way, too."

"Yes," Kirby said, "you'll only just make it. By the way, I've instructed the driver down there to keep you company to the airport. I thought you might feel happier."

Bliss conjured up a smile of relief. "As a matter of fact, I will. Thanks a lot."

"Do you mind if I hang on here for a few minutes? I gave the Yard this number and I'm expecting a call."

"Not a bit, Inspector. Just pull the door behind you when you leave." Bliss put on his raincoat, checked that he'd got his passport and tickets, and turned to Kirby for the last time. "Well—we did quite a job together, didn't we?"

"We did indeed," Kirby said. "I really am most grateful to you."

"Ah—*you* were the birdwatcher," Bliss said. "If I could, I'd promote you for that." He held out his hand. "Good-bye, Inspector. Thanks for all your help. I'll send you a postcard when we get settled."

"Do that, sir. Maybe I'll come and split a bottle of that Romanée Conti with you on my next holiday. If I ever get another, that is!" The phone rang. "Ah, there's my call."

"See you!" Bliss said. He raised his hand in salutation and went quickly downstairs. Sixty seconds later he was on his way to Lydd.

Corinne drove the van at a steady pace along the Dover road, keeping a careful eye on the traffic and the road surface. She was glad to be on the move again. The hour of waiting by herself, not knowing what was happening at Bampton Gardens, not knowing how the loading was getting on, had been a strain. But once on the road, with Banda safely in the back, her anxieties had melted away. Now she was in a confident and exhilarated mood.

She no longer felt even a trace of apprehension about the gang. Sergeant Groves and the other man had been positive they hadn't been followed, and her own observations in the mirror confirmed it. She'd been relieved to hear, too, that Mike was having an escort. Olsen and his friends were a worry she could finally put out of her mind.

Driving the van had presented no problems, thanks to the homework she'd done at the Blue Boar. She had mastered the gears in the first few minutes, the headlights were excellent, and the steering wasn't nearly as heavy as she'd expected. She knew the route to Dover from earlier journeys and scarcely had to look at the signs. Her ticket, money, passport and papers were in her bag, her suitcase and the Queen Anne table wedged against the chest behind her. Everything was under control. Her thoughts were already racing ahead to a smiling dawn in France, a triumphant meeting with Mike. What a celebration they'd have!

Her only slight concern was about Banda's comfort. There hadn't been a peep out of him, but he must be having a horrible time, shut up in that box with no room to move and straws in his hair and only a thin crack to breathe through. She'd have hated it herself. And there'd been one or two bad bumps on a stretch of road that was under repair. Perhaps she ought to check.

Just beyond Wrotham she pulled in to an empty lay-by and stopped the engine. She leaned back, and tapped on the chest. "Are you all right, Mr. Banda?"

The fastening clicked and the lid opened slightly. "Yes . . . Is there some trouble?"

"No—I just wanted to make sure you were still alive!"

"I am quite comfortable, thank you. Better than I expected. And I have taken two sleeping pills. You need not worry about me any more."

"Good."

The lid went down, the catch clicked. Corinne drove on, reassured. She could now give her undivided attention to the traffic and the timing of her arrival at Dover. She didn't want to get there too early, and have to hang about; she certainly mustn't be late.

In fact, her timing was perfect. She reached the Eastern Docks at a quarter to two, forty-five minutes before the ferry was due to sail. The queue of waiting cars was just beginning to move. She joined the line. As she approached the customs building she was aware of a quickening pulse. She must be ready to put on a good act. If by any chance Banda's disappearance had been discovered and the ports notified, even a VIP traveler could expect some attention. . . . But she had no trouble. Officialdom was at its friendliest. The immigration officer in his glass box waved her on with a smile and scarcely a glance at her extended passport. So did the people in the customs shed. The man who collected her tickets saluted her as though she were royalty. The way had certainly been prepared. She drove on down the ramp and parked in the car bay. She had to leave the van unlocked, an unbreakable rule, but she wasn't worried—she'd never heard of anyone interfering with cars during crossing. No sound came from the chest, and she guessed Banda was sleeping. The best thing he could do . . . She gathered up her coat and handbag and made her way to the top deck. The night was warm and still. She lit a cigarette and strolled slowly up and down the deck, looking at the harbor lights and stopping occasionally to watch the men preparing for departure in the bows.

The ship was a little late in leaving, but once on its way it made good time in as smooth a sea as anyone could have wished for.

Bliss, having boarded his plane with no fuss and little formality, passed the uneventful twenty-minute journey to Le Touquet considering the moves that would follow his rendezvous with Corinne and the freeing of Banda.

They'd all be pretty tired after the strain of the escape and a night without sleep, but five o'clock in the morning would be no time to go to a hotel. Anyway, Bliss wanted to push on southward as quickly as possible. Better if they found some quiet spot off the road, he thought, and had a doss in the car and the van for an hour or two. After that, a cleanup for Banda and, yes, maybe he ought to pay a morning visit to some barber, to get those long locks of his shorn and smoothed down before the hue and cry for him spread to the Continent. There'd be a bit of shopping to be done, too, some luggage for him, clothes. . . . And, of course, the second letter of instruction must be got off to his Zurich bank.

Then, a full day's drive, and an early night in a good hotel—Banda wearing his false mustache and glasses and beginning to settle into his new life as Harold Lever.

By easy stages, after that, to Aix-en-Provence. A check at the Crédit Lyonnais to see if confirmation of the second money transfer had come through. And if it had, farewell to Banda.

Yes—that seemed a reasonable program.

As the car ferry approached Boulogne, Corinne took a final look at her map of northern France. She and Bliss had arranged to meet on the Paris road, just south of a village called Vron. She checked the distances. Twenty-five kilometers from Boulogne to Montreuil, then another ten to Vron. Certainly not more than half an hour's run, even at a pace slow enough to avoid jolting Banda. Say forty-five minutes altogether, including getting off the ship. A mere nothing. And only one more hurdle.

The loudspeakers crackled. A voice from the bridge invited passengers to go to their cars. Corinne gathered up her things and joined the chattering throng descending to the car deck. Engines were already being throttled up there. A light bump against the dock side showed that the ship had arrived. Corinne climbed into the van and glanced back at the chest and baggage. Everything was in order. She started the engine. The line of cars began to roll. Now for the hurdle, getting ashore.

In fact, she had no trouble at all. The French port officials proved as eager to wave her on as the British had been. Smiles and salutes accompanied her to the gate. Kirby had evidently worked his spell again. By a quarter past four she had threaded her way through the Boulogne docks and was heading southwest along Route Nationale 1.

She drove very slowly at first, allowing all the other passengers from the ship to go by. It wouldn't do to have G.B. cars streaming past when Banda emerged from the chest. One by one, the red lights of the tourists faded into the distance. At that hour there was almost no other traffic. Very soon, Corinne was alone.

Or almost alone. It wasn't until she'd covered about ten kilometers that she began to wonder about a car that stayed persistently behind her. On the long straight stretches of the Route Nationale it could have passed her with ease at any time, but it hadn't attempted to. When she slowed for lights or traffic signs, it slowed too. When she put on speed, it held its distance. She continued to watch it uneasily in the mirror. Of course, some drivers never passed anything at night if they could help it. This man could be one of those. Probably she was imagining things again. All the same, she didn't like him on her tail. She slowed right down, almost to a crawl. Now he'd *have* to pass her. But he didn't. The gap remained unchanged.

Corinne was really worried now. All her old fears about the gang came surging back. Was it possible, in spite of Kirby's precautions, that Olsen's friends had somehow managed to keep track of what was happening, and had followed her to France? She didn't see how they could have—and anyway, why *her?* It was Mike they had a grudge against, and they could have followed him just as easily. Except, of course, that he'd had a police escort, and she hadn't. That could be it. They could be taking the path of least resistance. Following her, knowing that she'd lead them to Bliss. Hoping to settle their own score in a quiet spot, with no police around.

By now, Corinne was in a state of near-panic. The car was still on her tail. In a few minutes she'd be at the rendezvous. She must do something. Turn off somewhere. Try and give her pursuer the slip . . .

She was just entering Montreuil. It was a small nodal town of tortuous streets, a center with many exits. She'd noticed that on the map. And the men in the car couldn't know which exit she was going to take, where she was making for. It was the one place between her and the rendezvous where she could hope to throw off pursuit. She switched off her headlights and put on speed. Where the Paris road curved sharply to the right, she swung sharp left with a squeal of brakes. Almost at once she saw a side road opening on the right. The fingerpost said "Fruges." She turned along it and gave the van all it had, unmindful now of Banda. The road was a minor one, narrow and deserted. As she left the town, a wood loomed up ahead, with a verge and an open track into the trees. She swung the van in, doused all her lights and switched off the engine.

She wondered if she should rouse Banda and get him out of the chest, in case she needed help. Not that he'd be much use. . . . She looked back toward Montreuil. Everything seemed quiet. The minutes slipped by and nothing happened. Slowly her panic passed. Probably she'd scared herself for nothing. She felt rather ashamed. Mike had been right to doubt her in a crisis—at least where personal safety was concerned. What a flap! Anyhow, there was no danger now—the other car had long since gone on its way. Presently she set off again, retracing her route back to Montreuil and turning again along the Paris road. She ran through Vron and began to watch her distance indicator.

Three kilometers out of Vron—that was what they'd agreed. At a crossroad . . . She must be coming to it. Yes, there was the crossroad sign. She rounded a bend. The lights of a stationary car shone red by the roadside. She slowed beside it, saw it was the Mercedes, and turned the van in on the verge in front of it.

Bliss came to meet her, unhurriedly, a huge grin splitting his face. "Good show, darling!" He gave her a hug. "So we've pulled it off!"

"Yes . . ." After all the excitement, Corinne suddenly felt very tired.

"I expected you earlier. What held you up?"

"The boat was late starting, and then I thought someone was following me." Corinne described her small adventure.

Bliss smiled and put an arm reassuringly around her shoulders. "You imagined it, old thing, no one could possibly have kept track of us." He turned to the van. "Well, I suppose we'd better release the financial wizard."

"He's been asleep most of the time," Corinne said. "He took the pills. There hasn't been a sound from him since we landed."

"H'm—pity we can't keep it that way! I bet he'll start complaining as soon as he wakes up. . . ." Bliss opened the back of the van. "Now if this was a thriller, Inspector Kirby would pop out."

"Don't *say* such things!"

Bliss laughed, and tapped on the lid. "Open up, Banda, you've arrived. . . ." He broke off. "That's funny—the fastening's undone."

He raised the lid and looked in. Except for the straw, the chest was empty!

For a moment Bliss just stared down at it, shocked, uncomprehending, motionless. Then, as the bitter truth dawned, his hands clenched, his face grew pale with anger. He said slowly, with a venom Corinne had never heard in his voice before, "Why—the lousy bloody cheat!"

Corinne was staring down, too, scarcely able to believe her eyes. "I don't understand. . . . I talked to him on the way down. He was there when I drove onto the boat."

"Sure he was," Bliss said. "But not when you drove off. He got out during the crossing, when the car bay was deserted."

"But he'd taken sleeping pills. . . ."

"No, he hadn't—he just said he had, to lull you. He probably had the whole thing planned from the beginning. That's why he was so anxious not to be locked in the chest. He lay doggo till everyone had gone, let himself out, mixed with the passengers who hadn't got cars, and went ashore in the ordinary way with his new passport. He'd got the mustache and glasses with him—he'd have had no trouble."

"But . . . *why?*"

"So he wouldn't have to pay us the dough, of course. Don't you see, he's cleared off! Disappeared! He's two hundred thousand pounds richer than he should be, and we're two hundred thousand pounds poorer. What a bloody crook!"

Corinne stood for a moment in dazed silence. Then she said, "I suppose we should have thought of it."

"You're dead right, we should. Or *I* should. I could kick myself. All that effort!" Bliss groaned. "Think of it! All those weeks of planning, all the work we put in, all the risks we took. And for nothing! I must have been out of my mind."

"We've got the twenty-five thousand," Corinne said.

Bliss gave a grunt of disgust. "What's twenty-five thousand when you've banked on a fortune? Chicken feed!"

"It's better than nothing. . . . Anyway, what are we going to do?"

Bliss shrugged. "What *can* we do? Accept that we've failed, and try something else, I suppose. Collect the dough from Aix and push on to the south—I might get a few ideas on the Riviera. . . . One thing's for sure—we'll never find Banda now he's loose on the Continent."

"I suppose not," Corinne said slowly.

Dawn was just breaking. It was a beautiful morning, still and peaceful, but neither of the ex-conspirators was in a state to appreciate it. Bliss said, "We'd better decide on a route. I'll get the map," and went moodily to the Mercedes. Corinne stayed by the van, staring down at the ground.

Suddenly she called out. "Mike, wait a minute! I've remembered something."

Bliss half turned. "Oh? What?"

"I think perhaps I know where we could find Banda."

He was with her in a flash. "You *do*?"

"Yes, it's just come back to me. He was talking about it when I was driving him to London. I wasn't paying much attention at the time, but now I remember. He's got a villa in Menton. The Villa Hirondelle. He said he thought he'd go there and rest for a bit."

"Really?"

"He was terribly enthusiastic about the place. He described it to me—it sounded wonderful. I'm pretty sure he *will* go."

Bliss's face cleared. "Well, that's a break, I must say." Then he frowned. "But why on earth should he tell you? It was a pretty dim thing to do, if he knew he was going to clear off without paying us."

Corinne looked up at him, her eyes wide and innocent. "He had some silly idea I might join him there."

"Join him! You mean he expected you to keep quiet about where he was going when he didn't show up? Just ditch me, and switch to him?"

Corinne nodded. "He naturally didn't say that, but I can see, now, that it must have been in his mind."

"Well, he was certainly taking a big chance. I'm surprised he had the nerve. The fat slob! Imagine *you* joining *him* . . . !" Bliss gave a hoot of laughter at the idea. Then the laughter died. He eyed Corinne with sudden suspicion. "Wait a minute . . . ! Is that why you didn't tell me about Menton right away? You were thinking of going!"

"Of course not, Mike—don't be ridiculous."

"I bet the thought crossed your mind."

"If it did," Corinne said, "it crossed straight back again. I'd sooner share two hundred thousand with you than millions with Banda."

Bliss grinned. "I like you too! Okay—consider yourself acquitted. So we're in business again!"

"Yes . . . What shall we do—go straight to Menton?"

"As straight as the road'll take us," Bliss said. "We'll

find that old goat and pin his ears back and damn well collect our dues."

With the map spread out on the bonnet of the Mercedes, they made their plans for the eight-hundred-mile journey.

"Speed's the main thing," Bliss said. "If Banda took the train at Boulogne he could be in Menton by tomorrow morning, and we want to reach him before he has a chance to change his mind and move on. So I suggest we get rid of the van, which is slow anyway, and take turns driving the Mercedes and sleeping. That way we'll have covered five or six hundred miles by tonight, and we should get to the villa early tomorrow afternoon, soon after Banda. How's that with you?"

Corinne nodded. "As long as I can sleep first."

"Sure. Now about the route. We can bypass Paris. It saves hours and I've been over the course before. After that I think we'd better stick to the R.N.7."

Corinne agreed. "It's not the pleasantest way, but it's the fastest road. I drove over it last summer."

Bliss folded up the map. "With a friend, no doubt?"

Corinne gave a rather weary smile. "Naturally," she said.

They left the van at the first garage they found open, a place in Amiens. They might return for it later, Bliss told the proprietor, or they might decide to sell it—they'd write and say which. Bliss transferred their personal luggage to the Mercedes, but didn't bother about anything else. The chest was too big to take, the books were of no special interest, and Corinne said she'd never particularly cared for the Queen Anne table, which was a rather poor fake. They made a quick breakfast of croissants and coffee at a restaurant opposite the garage and by eight-thirty were on the road again, heading south at high speed.

Corinne slept till Fontainebleau and took over when they reached the R.N.7. Bliss snoozed till Angers. To save time they bought food and a little wine for lunch and picnicked briefly by the roadside. The Mercedes was running perfectly, and the sheer speed of their passage through the country was exhilarating. Their only delay was north of Lyons, where farmers with a grievance were staging some sort of demonstration, but the Mercedes with its G.B. plate was soon waved on. They passed three pile-ups, but had no near-misses themselves. They talked very little. Both were concentrating on the driving and the goal. Both were wondering if they really would find Banda at the end of the road. But their expectations were high, their spirits good. The weather was steadily improving, the southern countryside looked bright and cheerful. There were terra-cotta roofs now, tables out-of-doors, striped umbrellas, roses and lilac in bloom. The vine-covered slopes, hot and dry under a vivid blue sky, seemed to offer a foretaste of all the pleasures they had planned.

By evening they were at Valence, with most of their journey done. They spent a restful night there and left early in the morning, refreshed and eager for the confrontation. They reached Menton at three in the afternoon, well up to schedule. Bliss stopped to get directions at the post office, and turned the car toward Cap Martin.

The sea was as blue as Banda had said it would be. The promontory, with its pine trees and orange groves and luxurious white villas, fully justified the description he'd given of it. The Villa Hirondelle, when they finally located it high up on the cliffside, was a sparkling delight.

Bliss parked the car by the gate, got out, and peered ahead through the bushes that lined the drive. There was a moment of anxious silence. Then he turned, smiling, and gave Corinne the thumbs-up sign. "It's okay—he's there! I can see a window open, and there's a pair of swimming trunks drying on the terrace. Oh, boy, are we going to surprise him!"

Corinne had started to apply lipstick. "What do you think he'll say?"

"Oh, he'll make up some yarn, I shouldn't wonder. How he couldn't stand being in the chest any longer, and didn't want to startle you by suddenly appearing, and decided it would be safer if he simply cleared off on his own. How he was going to write to me at my bank in Aix and say where he was so we could come and collect the money!"

Corinne laughed softly. "That sounds more like you than Banda." She finished making up her face. "Right, I'm ready. Don't forget that if a maid or someone comes to the door, you ask for Monsieur George Wilson."

They left the car and walked slowly up the drive. Bliss tried to see through the window, but the villa was built up on piles and nothing was visible from the ground. Somewhere inside the house, a radio was playing. They reached the front door and Bliss rang the bell. They waited. After a moment, the radio went off. Footsteps sounded in the hall. The door opened.

There were several men in the hall. One was a uniformed gendarme. Two others had the watchful air of plain-clothes policemen. But it was at the fourth man that Bliss and Corinne stared in horror—the man who'd opened the door.

It was Inspector Kirby.

"Hullo, Miss Lake. Afternoon, Mr. Bliss." Kirby stepped back invitingly. "Do come in—we've been expecting you."

Shocked and speechless, Bliss and Corinne followed him like automatons into a large sitting room.

"Find yourselves chairs," Kirby said. "Make yourselves comfortable. We've a lot to talk about."

They sat down. Kirby took a seat opposite them. The three French policemen disposed themselves in a half circle, as though for a performance.

"Well, Mr. Bliss?"

There was a short, unhappy silence. Then Bliss gave a faint shrug, a shrug of surrender. For a wild moment at the door, he'd wondered if he could bluff. Words had formed in his mind—stalling words like, "Well, fancy meeting you, Inspector," while he tried to think up a story, but they'd been too idiotic to say. Obviously, the game was up. Nothing but complicity could explain how he and Corinne happened to be calling on a criminal who'd just escaped from England. Nothing but full possession of the facts could explain the presence of Kirby at the villa.

"I assume you know everything," Bliss said.

Kirby nodded.

"Have you got Banda?"

"Yes, Mr. Bliss, we've got him. Safe and sound."

"I should have guessed. He'd never have had the

guts to clear off like that. . . . So this is the end of our beautiful friendship?"

"I'm afraid so, sir."

"What happened, Inspector? How did you find out?"

"Well," Kirby said, "the fact is you talked too much."

"Talked too much? About what?"

"About wine, sir . . . Remember that day you gave me the ice wine? And told me about your modest cellar —your cool cupboard? Well, after you left me at the flat and I'd finished my phone talk I went round the place putting lights out and closing doors, and I happened to stick my head inside your cupboard. It was so warm in there I could hardly believe it was the one you'd meant, but the wine racks fixed to the wall showed it was. I took the liberty of moving a thermometer from the kitchen to the cupboard. Do you know what the temperature was? Seventy-five degrees. And do you know why? There are hot-water pipes running under that floor. It couldn't ever be anything but an oven."

Bliss gave a resigned nod. "I get it. . . . Go on, Hawkeye!"

"Well, sir, I was naturally very puzzled. I remembered you'd mentioned fifty-five degrees as the right temperature for wine, so that cupboard didn't make sense. Anyway, I rang up our Assistant Commissioner, who's also a bit of a wine fancier, and asked him if anyone who knew about wine would store a choice vintage like your Romanée Conti in a temperature of seventy-five degrees. He said not unless the fellow was a lunatic."

"And you knew I wasn't a lunatic," Bliss said.

"Exactly, sir. So now I began to wonder about the

contents of that chest of yours. If you hadn't taken
four dozen bottles of Romanée Conti, what had you
taken? Naturally, I'd no idea of the truth, but I thought
possibly you were smuggling some valuables out—
stolen property—something like that. Otherwise, why
the big pretense? So I phoned Dover C.I.D., described
the van, and asked them to take a look. They went
aboard the ferry, and they found Banda."

Bliss grinned. "That must have shaken one and all!"

"It certainly shook me, Mr. Bliss, when they told me
—there hadn't even been a report that he was missing.
It also left me with a problem, which I had to resolve
pretty fast as the ship was already behind schedule.
Obviously I could have had Miss Lake arrested there
and then, but I was much more concerned to get you.
And I didn't know where you were—by that time you'd
have left Le Touquet. I didn't know, either, where the
two of you had arranged to meet, and I did Miss Lake
the honor of thinking that even if she were arrested
she wouldn't necessarily tell me. All I did know was
that if Miss Lake didn't turn up at the rendezvous,
you'd realize something was wrong and probably disappear for good. So I did a bit of phoning across the
Channel, and the French police agreed to tail Miss
Lake's van to the meeting place and hold you both
until I arrived. Unfortunately, by a piece of—er—bad
luck, they lost her."

"That's right," Bliss said, "she was playing hard to
get! But you'd still got Banda, of course. I suppose he
talked."

Kirby gave a deprecatory smile. "Well, sir, Mr.
Banda isn't one of the toughest characters I've come
across, and he was under some pressure. There was

the question of additional charges that might or might not be brought against him. Not that any inducement was held out to him, of course, but the matter *was* lightly touched on. The prospect of an even longer sentence than the one he's likely to get obviously didn't appeal to him—so, as you say, he talked. Very fast and very comprehensively. In fact, he gave us the whole story."

"The rat," Bliss said, without heat.

Kirby gave a sympathetic nod. "Strictly between ourselves, sir, I rather share your view. Anyhow, once I knew he'd intended to come to Menton, and that he'd mentioned to Miss Lake he intended to come, it wasn't difficult to work out your next moves. Obviously you'd think he'd double-crossed you when you found the chest empty—obviously you'd come rushing down here, full of righteous indignation, to collect your money. It was just a question of boarding a plane, enlisting the cooperation of my good French colleagues, and waiting till you arrived. And that, I think, puts you completely in the picture."

There was a little silence. Then Bliss said, "Well, it would be churlish of me not to congratulate you, Inspector. You did a magnificent job."

"Thank you, sir . . . Possibly, as a policeman, I ought not to say this, but I've never before come across a plan of such extraordinary ingenuity, or rogues I was more reluctant to apprehend. Apart from your one small bit of carelessness, the whole thing was brilliantly executed. . . . It's none of my business, but it does seem to me a great pity that you and Miss Lake didn't employ your talents and your charm in some more worthwhile direction. You would obviously have been very successful in many legitimate fields."

"I dare say," Bliss said, with a wry smile. "But it wouldn't have been nearly such fun, would it? Well, there it is—a fair cop! What happens now?"

"The French authorities will accommodate you both tonight—separately, I'm afraid. Tomorrow we shall fly home, and you'll both be charged."

"What precisely will the charges be?"

"As far as you're concerned, sir? Oh—attempting to pervert the course of justice—obtaining a passport by false pretenses—forgery—conspiracy—arson. . . . A few things like that . . . You asked me once, Mr. Bliss, if I could guarantee your safety for ten years. I think, now, I can do that."

"Very decent of you," Bliss said. "Would it help, do you suppose, if I were to hand over the twenty-five thou. that Banda paid me?"

"Well, it wouldn't do any harm, sir. I'd certainly recommend it."

"Are you likely to get the rest of Banda's money?"

"As a matter of fact, we are. He always denied that he'd salted anything away, but now, of course, he's had to admit it. I think that with a little more pressure he'll hand the lot over. It's rather ironical, really. His former shareholders should be quite grateful to you."

"Unfortunately they won't be on the jury," Bliss said.

"No."

"And what about Corinne?"

"Oh, she'll probably be charged with aiding and abetting. A serious offense, in view of what she abetted —but I don't doubt she was very much under your influence."

"Yes, I think she was." Bliss got up and went over to Corinne. She was pale, but composed. "I'm terribly sorry," he said. "I made a frightful hash of it all." He bent and kissed her—for the first time with a little tenderness. "I guess I was too damned sure of myself."

She forced a smile. "Don't worry—I can take it."

"They say Holloway is a very comfortable prison. But no men, I'm afraid!"

"I'll survive."

"You'll be out long before I am. You could drop me a line if you ever felt like it."

"I might," she said. "Where to?"

"Oh, care of H.M. Prisons—they'll always know where to find me!" Bliss turned away. "Okay, Inspector —we're all yours."

V

In his cell in Wormwood Scrubs, three weeks and a sensational trial later, Bliss sat thinking.

His thoughts were not wholly black. For one thing, old Hawkeye had been wrong about the sentence. Three years was very different from ten. Two years, with remission for good conduct—and Bliss would be a model prisoner. What Kirby hadn't reckoned on— though he should have, knowing his man—was the impression Bliss had made while pleading "Guilty." That short, modest speech of his—so carefully rehearsed and memorized, so apparently straight from a boyish heart —had been a triumph. . . . Sorry to have done it, of course. Realized it was wrong. Fact was it had appealed to him as an exciting adventure. Pitting his wits and skill against authority. Sort of challenge. True, he'd done it to earn money as well, but a man racing single-handed in a small boat across the Atlantic might have his eye on the prize as well as the struggle. And at least he hadn't harmed anybody, except Miss Lake. His greatest regret was involving her in the escapade. He took full responsibility. He'd suggested the plot and he'd made all the running. He realized now he'd exploited her affection for him. She'd been most reluc-

tant to start with, but he'd persuaded her. He did hope
the court would be lenient with her. And that was it.
He'd never been in trouble before—didn't intend ever
to be again. But he recognized that he owed society a
debt and he was ready to take his medicine. Yes, it
had been a brilliant performance. The judge had
seemed quite touched. Must have been, to believe in
it!

So there was still a future. Maybe a different sort of
future. Bliss had given some thought to that aspect.
Once you started getting caught, conning was like
gambling—a mug's game. With a police record, it
would be asking for trouble to go on. And he didn't
have to. Kirby had been quite right—there *were* all
sorts of legitimate jobs that would suit his talents. Bit
late now to become a lawyer, though he'd have been a
dab hand at cooking up plausible defenses in hopeless
cases. Or a clergyman—fantastic the line of chat they
got away with. Or a politician—the greatest con men
of the lot . . . All too late—but there'd be other
opportunities.

Maybe even with Corinne. She'd be out of jail in
nine months, and he didn't think she bore him any
grudge. Odd how he'd come to like that girl. Quite
seriously. Missed her companionship. Never thought
he would . . .

So things weren't so bad, really. He began to hum
softly to himself—"There Is a Happy Land Far, Far
Away." . . . The fact was he'd got off very lightly.
Nemesis had only done half a job.

Sounds in the corridor outside brought his reflections
to an end. Cell doors were beginning to slam. Exercise

time. Bliss got up from his settle and moved toward the door.

He fell into line with the other prisoners and marched out into the exercise yard. As he walked, he accidentally trod on the heel of the man in front of him. The man turned around. He had bulging cheek-bones and big ears and pale eyes, as friendly as a rattlesnake's. It was Jack Olsen.

He looked hard at Bliss. Slowly a grin spread across his face from big ear to big ear—the most diabolical grin Bliss had ever seen.

"Well if it isn't Bright Boy!" Olsen said. He flexed his giant muscles. "You and me must do some exercises together!"